PRINCES

OF

THE

UNIVERSE

Cover Artist: Natasha Snow Designs

Editing: Proof Positive

Proofreading: Judy's Proofreading

Formatting: Rainbow Danger Designs

Paperback: 978-1-9994727-5-7

Ebook: 978-1-9994727-4-0

For Fynnian.

In any universe
  You are my dark star

YOUNG THE GIANT, "SUPERPOSITION"

ONE

ELI

S TRUCTURE WAS A TRICKY THING. There was a fine line between having a plan and succumbing to monotony. I wasn't above admitting that my life had become increasingly predictable. It wasn't that I lacked forward momentum, and I didn't think it was at all a negative thing. I got off to what you could call a rocky start and managed to find a sense of peace with my routine. Every morning I'd wake up at quarter to six, walk my dog, Prince, go to work, go for a run with Prince, eat dinner, and watch TV or read until bed. Occasionally I'd get dragged out by Aoibheann, the only person I'd consider a friend. We ate lunch together every day at the office and talked about everything—well, she talked and I listened. For the sake of simplicity, she went by Eve at work, for which I was grateful. She worried about me being lonely, but I assured her on numerous occasions that I was just fine. Fine—the wrong word to use when talking to a woman.

It wasn't a lie, though. I'd tried my hand at dating over the years, and it always ended in disaster. Nearly every woman I'd ever been with would break things off after a couple of months, saying they didn't feel a connection. Some even told me straight up that I couldn't love. After all I'd been through, I honestly didn't think they were wrong. I gave everything I had to Prince, but a connection like that with another person had never come. I'd resigned myself that it never would and gave up the pretense of dating a couple of years ago. Since then, I'd fallen into my comfortable routine, and I'd been happier for it. Dating was a mess for me. I did try, but it wasn't enough for any partner I'd ever had.

I stopped for a coffee on my way to work that day. I usually brewed it at home, but I left my travel mug in the staff lounge the day before. Money wasn't tight, and I didn't have any frivolous hobbies, so treating myself to an eight-dollar coffee and a muffin once in a while wouldn't kill me. I grabbed a cupcake with sprinkles for Eve since she had a penchant for all things sugar.

I got to work with fifteen minutes to spare before the official start of the day and used that time to start the daily crossword puzzle in the paper. Red Right Hand was a relatively trendy ad agency founded a few years ago. The whole place had a laid-back, hipster vibe to promote creativity, and it did work. Floor-to-ceiling windows lined the right wall of the industrial-turned-commercial rectangular space, offering all the natural light one could ever ask for—but we usually kept the shades half drawn to avoid glare—while offices and boardrooms were on the left. The reception area at the front was small but had comfortable leather seating in a shade of red that matched our bold logo. Down at the back wall was the "creative space"; one could find several geometric book-shelves full of novels, magazines, and design books, as well as beanbag chairs, another leather couch, a couple of small white tables, and a bigger table repurposed from a wooden door in front of the couch. The main working space was wide open with oak-topped desks on metal legs painted white. If I had to guess, I'd say those were from repurposed materials too. Each desk was home to two Mac desktops, one on either side. I lucked out when I was hired eighteen months ago and was placed with Eve—a spirited auburn-haired Irish woman a few years my senior.

Her monitor faced the entrance, allowing her to easily track my approach every morning. I was always greeted with a half-cocked smile and kind blue eyes, framed by thin brown-rimmed glasses. Today was no different.

"Mornin', Eli. Howya?"

"Good morning." I held up the branded bag with the cupcake and bit back a grin as her smile got toothy and wide. "Got you a little something."

I handed the bag over to her outstretched grabby-hands and sat down in my chair, not quite able to stifle my laughter a second time. She tore into the bag and beamed up at me.

"Sprinkles. You know me so well. I'd marry ya if you'd have me, you know."

I shook my head and sipped my coffee. "It's an enticing offer, but I'd only disappoint you. Besides, I don't think Samir would appreciate you marrying me suddenly." They were engaged to be wed in a few months.

"Sam fancies you a lot. The three of us could be very happy together," she said with a wink. That type of flirty behavior would normally unnerve me, but it was the status quo with Eve and it didn't faze me in the least.

"Hmm. Tempting—I'm not into guys, though. Perhaps dating would be easier if I was."

Eve rolled her chair around to the side of the desk, closing the distance between us. She wore a dark green dress and black kitten heels and had a white blazer slung over the back of her chair. "You're not into anyone, it seems. Have you ever given fellas a go to see if that's the answer?" she asked quietly.

I jerked my head back and said, "No," way too fast. I

mentally kicked myself as I saw a hint of suspicion flash over Eve's eyes. The truth was that, yes, I *had* been with a guy before. Sexually, but not romantically. I was eighteen, in a bad place, and in need of cash. Fate pissed on me, and I was presented with the opportunity to get some quick cash from doing porn. With no other options, I agreed to it—which was a huge mistake. I knew with absolute certainty that it wasn't an experience I wanted to relive, and I had tried my best not to think about it over the last ten years.

I wasn't that scared, helpless kid anymore. The present me sure wasn't anything to brag about, but I no longer felt helpless. Or hopeless. The whole issue with my love life hardly registered when I looked at the bigger picture of my life, the different strokes and colors all blended to create the man I'd become.

"Whatever you say, pet." Eve rolled back around to her side of the shared desk and took a bite from the top of the cupcake, joy instantly overtaking her soft features.

I sighed inwardly, relieved that she didn't pursue what I knew was a joking line of questioning. We settled into our lazy morning ritual of drinking coffee and checking our emails and messages, sharing any good news or gossip that came up. It was bound to be a busy day, being the first day back after the Fourth of July long weekend. I'd celebrated by curling up on the couch with Prince resting her head on my knee and watched *Independence Day*. Eve had tried to get me to go with her and Sam to his parents' cottage, but I politely declined, not wanting to intrude.

About twenty minutes later, our boss, Andrea, swung by and requested that I sit in on a pitch in the Prescott room, the largest boardroom we had, starting in fifteen minutes. Considering I was still the newest team member, having me sit in on meetings and a pitch wasn't unheard of, it just hadn't happened in several months. I had my own clients now and was producing steady work for the agency, so the request struck me as odd, but not enough for me to question it. Eve and I exchanged a series of cocked eyebrows and head-shakes then I gathered up a notepad and a pen to give my hands something to do and headed into the Prescott room, taking a seat next to Andrea.

"What's going on today?" I asked, smoothing out the wrinkles in my light blue plaid dress shirt. The laid-back atmosphere meant I could dress however I wanted, so long as it was neat and not offensive, though I still opted for dress shirts more often than not. Eve opened my eyes to short-sleeved button-ups in the summer, which were a lifesaver on hot days. I still wasn't sold on cuffing the sleeves, but she assured me it was the right thing to do. No matter how hot it got, I couldn't bring myself to wear shorts to work.

"We have an important potential client coming in, and I wanted fresh faces at the table. This is also a good opportunity for you to see me personally handle a pitch," Andrea replied with a wink.

Shit. "They must be important."

She nodded, sending her blonde curls bouncing, and slid a file over to me as a few more agents entered the room and sat on the other side of the table. "Bryan Rettger. Youngest son of Malcolm Rettger—owner and operator of the highly lucrative Rettger Homestead Ranch down in Texas. He's coming in today in relation to a private venture."

I nodded, immediately understanding why she was so excited. If we made an impression with him, it could potentially lead to working with his father, which would be huge for any company, let alone one as small as Red Right Hand. "I see. I'll keep quiet and take notes."

"You're a fast learner, Elijah," she teased, gently jabbing me in the ribs with her elbow. I smiled at her and reviewed the file she'd slid in front of me. Bryan Rettger was just a couple of years older than me at thirty, and was opening a retail bakery downtown. The space was leased, yet the business didn't have a name yet, let alone any marketing strategy or ideas of where to take it.

I was surprised to see that he'd already secured the space without having a concrete business model, but I'd never understood the whims of the elite. At five minutes to the hour, the door to the Prescott room opened, and the receptionist showed in a man in a fitted denim shirt over a white T-shirt, sage green cotton shorts that hit a couple of inches above the knee, and a pair of well-broken-in sandals—like, Birkenstocks, or whatever. He looked casual but clean and stylish in ways that I avoided. My eyes tracked back up his extremely broad-shouldered athletic figure to take in his face, and my stomach flipped, almost as hard as I felt like the room did. I knew this man, and the way he stared back at me confirmed that my worst fear had come to pass. A small half smile curled across his lips as his green eyes pinned me in place. Sweat prickled on my lower back as I did my best to regulate my breathing and not crumble under his gaze.

I looked away as Andrea stood and walked around me to greet him. Her musical voice was muddled to my ears behind the pounding of my own damn pulse, coming in fast and hard. The professional in me wouldn't allow rudeness in front of a potential client, so I pushed myself to my feet and forced a smile across my tight jaw.

"Bryan Rettger. Pleasure to meet you," he said as he held out his hand. His voice came out smooth and steady, and he'd schooled the half smile from his expression.

Bryan Rettger. I squared my shoulders and held my head up high, nearly looking him directly in the eyes as I extended my hand and shook his. "Elijah Harper. Ditto." Fuck—there went my sense of professionalism. Andrea side-eyed me like I'd lost my mind while Bryan blinked at me a few times before a smile softened his features. I glanced over at Andrea apologetically and saw the moment her shoulders relaxed as Bryan seemed utterly tickled by my response.

His gaze flicked down, the amused expression never leaving his face, and then came back up to meet mine with one raised eyebrow. Utterly confused, I cast my eyes down and was horrified to see that I was still holding his goddamn hand.

"Ah, I'm sorry, Mr. Rettger." I released his hand immediately and felt the tips of my ears burn hot, thankful for my thick, dark brown hair that was long enough to cover the tops of my ears.

"Please, call me Bryan," he replied lightly.

"Bryan." Bryan. The name felt so foreign and wrong to me. I knew this man from a lifetime ago. I knew him in a way I didn't know any other man. I knew him as my former scene partner from when I was a barely legal adult. I knew him as Rhett fucking Ryder.

TWO

BRYAN

WELL, I'LL BE DAMNED. Elijah was the last person I expected to see when I walked in for a pitch I was already planning on accepting. Red Right Hand was a promising new company, and they'd turned out some edgy work. I knew they were the agency I wanted to realize my vision for the bakery. Seeing Elijah again after all these years was an unexpected surprise. He looked a bit stricken upon seeing my face, which left me just as confused as I was a decade ago when I saw him last. Although I did find it odd that he used his real name for the shoot.

The pitch went as well as I'd expected it to. I was only half paying attention, unable to stop my eyes from wandering over to Elijah. He kept pretending he wasn't staring back at me, but I'd caught him several times. His hair was a lot shorter than it was before, and he was still lean—yet not skinny like he had been. Other than that, he looked exactly the same. Same feathered bangs slung across his forehead, same cute, flat mole on the left side of his jaw, same disarming brown eyes that were the perfect blend of cinnamon and caramel. They were the perfect almond shape too, lending him a soft expressiveness that stood out on his face. He wasn't what you'd consider delicate or pretty by any definition, but he was cute and adorable in a very unique way. In a cute yet hairy-guy kind of way. It was apparently a combination that worked for me, because I wanted to pin him against the nearest flat surface and reacquaint myself with the taste of his tongue—not to mention other body parts.

He had on a short-sleeved shirt, allowing me a glimpse of his lean arms I wasn't about to pass up. His shoulders were more squared than I remembered, and he looked all around more fit, though not in a bulky gym kind of way. I'd know, considering the gym was my go-to whenever I needed an escape that baking couldn't give me.

Andrea Wilcox finished her impressive presentation, drawing my attention away from Elijah and back to the reason I was actually there. She had some good ideas that I liked, but the overall plan was a bit more ambitious and far-reaching than what I'd narrowly had in mind. She spoke of expansion and brand and distribution, and she did so beautifully. Her passion and attention to detail were why I chose this particular agency, but the pitch was just a bit… extra. I gave her my best Sunday smile, and spared Elijah another glance, only to see that his brows were drawn together, and he didn't look happy about something—beyond my presence.

"That all sounds intriguing, Andrea," I started, choosing my words carefully. "It's a lot for me to consider, but I do like the work that's—" Movement in my periphery drew my attention back to Elijah, who was scrawling on his notepad, as he'd done several times during the presentation, while everyone else in the room had kept their undivided attention on their boss. "You know what… would I be able to have a private word with Mr. Harper?" He hadn't mentioned that I could address him by his first name, and I didn't want to make him any more uncomfortable than he already was.

To her credit, Andrea's professional veneer never faltered. She graciously conceded to my request without showing an ounce of unease at leaving her agent with what she clearly considered an important client. I was sure it had something to do with my family, but I'd learned long ago to get over feeling salty or ungrateful for it. The other agents wordlessly followed her out, and once the door clicked closed behind me, I turned my attention to Elijah. He straightened his back and faced me, looking ready for a fight.

"What do you want from me?" he asked.

I shook my head easily and raised my palms from the table without lifting my wrists. "It's not like that. I just want to hear your thoughts on the pitch." It wasn't entirely a lie. I was more interested in talking to him about personal matters, but that could wait. Work seemed like a safer topic and one that would hopefully let him relax.

"Oh," he replied, his shoulders losing their tension bit by bit. "I'm sorry. I just... forget it. Ah, the pitch. Andrea presented compelling and proven methods. I'm sure the campaign will be a success should you choose our agency."

"Relax and tell me what you really think. Is that how you'd do it?"

"No," he answered immediately and with unwavering certainty. I leaned forward, further onto the table, and twined my fingers in front of me while I waited for Elijah to continue. "It's a strong campaign, but it feels wrong for your company. I don't mean any disrespect, but a smaller... more grassroots approach would be a better fit, in my opinion. Gaining a loyal local following is going to be essential to your viability and success. The location is great; right on the cusp of reaching professionals on their commute and the hipster crowd. This big branding approach isn't going to appeal to them, though. Your file said that you were undecided on opening as a coffee shop that sold baked goods or a bakery that also offered coffee."

It wasn't a question, so I merely nodded and let him go. "Baking is your specialty, and the last thing downtown needs is another coffee place, so I think it would be prudent to keep the focus on your skills. Offering tea and a limited coffee selection will be an asset, but not the main draw. The focus needs to be on the community. Positive word of mouth is going to be the most beneficial advertising we can hope for, the rest will be to supplement that." He broke eye contact with me as soon as he finished his pitch, returning his attention to his notes.

"Damn. Okay."

Elijah tilted his head up at me, eyes narrowed slightly. "What do you mean, 'okay'?"

I smirked and shrugged as I stood up and opened the door, welcoming just Andrea back in. She reclaimed her seat and looked at me expectantly. "Thank you for indulging my request. After some consideration, I'd like to move forward with your agency."

A genuine smile lit up her face while Elijah's expression remained guarded. "That's fantastic news, Bryan. We're looking forward to crafting the best possible ad campaign for your business."

"About that," I started, licking my lips. "I would love for Mr. Harper to be the agent in charge." Elijah's eyes went wide, as did Andrea's. I probably shouldn't have said it, and just left him alone, but it was out now. I'd be lying if I said I didn't want to talk to him more—and I really did like all of his suggestions. I just needed to know what happened to him… why he disappeared.

After the initial surprise, she once again conceded to my request after giving Elijah instructions to report in once our time concluded. A silence descended on the room when she left, and I didn't want to be the first one to break it. Years of playing baseball gave me a patience I likely wouldn't have otherwise possessed. Waiting for the right pitch was a necessary skill—being impatient and swinging at the wrong time could cost you the game. If Elijah wanted to wait me out, we'd be here all damn afternoon.

"Why did you do that?" he finally asked. "Anyone working here could do this for you, and probably do it better."

"Mr. Harper—"

"Elijah is fine."

"Elijah," I amended, "perhaps any of your colleagues would do a bang-up job, but they're not the ones who sold me."

Elijah shook his head. "It doesn't have to be me."

"But it is." I liked his ideas. Yes, I liked him too, but that was secondary. I got up from the head of the table, walked around closer to Elijah, and leaned against the table. I gripped the edge of the table in favor of crossing my arms. "I'd like to discuss your vision further, but I do recognize that this is very"—I waved a hand in front of my chest —"spur of the moment." Elijah scoffed under his breath. I ignored it and carried on. "How long do you need to do… whatever it is you need to do before we can discuss the plan more?"

"A week to do some preliminary research should be enough. I'll also need to see the space. There were some pictures in your file, though seeing the space and the neighborhood will be beneficial for me. The sooner that happens, the sooner I can start my research."

"Okay. When works for you? I don't want to interfere with your other projects, so I'll work around your schedule," I offered.

Elijah closed the folder in front of him and sighed. "Today isn't good for me. I can do tomorrow or Thursday."

"During working hours?"

"Yes, of course."

I considered my options. I wanted to see him again as soon as possible, but I had a pick-up baseball game on Wednesday evening and I didn't want to be rushed with Elijah. Just in case. "Thursday is best for me. How about eleven? I can pick you up here if you'd like."

"I can take the train or a bus, thanks," he replied.

"Will you do me a favor and leave Thursday evening open as well? I'd like to see you outside of the context of work." *Clearly* we had some shit to talk about if we were to get rid of the awkward atmosphere between us. I figured Elijah would appreciate doing it off the clock, so as to not mix business with pleasure—so to speak.

His mouth opened, the word "no" already forming on his lips, but then he snapped it shut. After a few moments of watching his jaw tighten, he said he'd keep his evening clear and it took all of my self-control not to make a scene. I nodded and told him I'd get out of his hair until Thursday. I didn't want to leave, but it wasn't always about what I wanted. I'd have my chance to talk to him in a couple of days, and I wouldn't be greedy before then.

"Looking forward to what you can do for me," I said as I extended my hand.

Elijah stood and shook my hand before ducking out of the room with the folder clutched tight in his grasp. I didn't let myself appreciate how cute his ass looked in the fitted blue chinos he wore. Nope. And I definitely didn't look twice.

I went straight home after the meeting and was greeted by the usual sight of my roommate, blond hair a wild mess, in his boxers and a tank, typing away on his laptop at the kitchen island while bumping "Ice Ice Baby" through the surround sound. We had a perfectly fine kitchen table, but he liked to set up shop at the island sometimes—closest to the food with a direct line of sight to the TV, he'd say. He was a website programmer and worked a lot from home, loving the perks of being able to do so. Clearly.

"Hey, man," he called out without taking his eyes off his work. He suddenly stopped then looked up at me with narrowed eyes. "You're back pretty damn early. Meeting not go well?"

I tossed my keys onto the table by the door and made my way over to the kitchen to sit opposite Mac, facing the kitchen. He was a messy fucker in the kitchen and banned from doing any serious cooking, which suited him just fine. He kept the rest of our place immaculately clean, but the kitchen was *my* space. I decorated our kitchen and decked it out with high-end stainless steel appliances and wood countertops. The backsplash was tiled with gorgeous rustic bricks creating a style I hoped to replicate in my new bakery. I felt at home in this kitchen. Working in a place similar to it might cut down on the stresses of being a small-business owner. I hoped it would help, anyway.

"The meeting went great, actually." I leaned over the counter and propped myself up on my elbows. "Remember that awful bet we made in freshman year?"

Mac's face twisted into a shit-eating grin. "You mean when you foolishly bet against me like the noob you were and lost? Giving the world your short, but oh so memorable film career?"

I bowed my head once while a smile pulled at my lips. "That'd be the one."

"What of it? Are you planning on throwing a viewing party again?"

"First of all, it was *you* who threw the first one."

Mac held up his hands and shrugged. "Semantics."

"I don't think that means what you think it means."

"Whatever. Get on with your story, bruh."

"Anyway, I filmed a scene with this really shy, cute guy, Elijah—"

"Oh, yeah. I remember. He bailed on you or something," Mac said, sparing his laptop a quick glance.

"That's the one. So, I walked into the ad agency today and who do you think was sitting in the boardroom next to the boss?"

"Get the fuck out." My smile got wider, and I waggled my brows at him. "Fuck, you're serious. What the hell happened?"

I sighed and filled Mac in on the meeting, what I said to Elijah privately, and my plan for after I showed him the new space on Thursday, not skimming over any details. Mac was a lot of things, but he was my best friend and my confidant, and had been for more than a decade. He'd tell me if I was way off base or not.

"Does that sound okay?" I asked, tracing the wood grain under my fingertips.

"I think it's not going to go how you hope it will, Bry. I do hope I'm wrong, though. Just be prepared to accept that he might not change his mind or want to talk to you at all outside of what he has to for work. Your tall, dark, and handsome shtick might not be enough to make him *not* dread seeing you."

"It's not a shtick," I muttered.

"Whatever, dude. You're not usually broody, but if you keep on like this, you'll be the perfect lead for the next teen vampire blockbuster."

I rolled my eyes at him and rolled my shoulders. "You're

right. I'm not acting like myself. You hungry? I feel like cooking."

"Is that a serious question? Of course I am."

I stepped around Mac and shooed him away to the table by the bay windows. I pulled a bunch of fresh veggies out of the fridge aimlessly and started dicing and julienning to clear my mind. I felt eyes on me and turned my attention back to Mac for a moment, not surprised to see his brown eyes watching me.

"You're so wifey material when you get like this, dude."

I couldn't contain my smile and conceded to Mac's infectious good mood as he cranked up the volume on "Jump Around."

THREE

ELI

I FINISHED THE REST OF MY DAY with an unfocused mind. Avoidable mistakes were made as a result, which only frustrated me further. The worried glances Eve sent my way told me she knew something was bothering me, but she left me alone. This wasn't something I could talk to her about —or anyone.

My second-worst memory had been brought back to light, and I was in panic mode. And worse? Rhe—*Bryan* was potentially blackmailing me into doing God-knows-what with him after our meeting. I didn't need him to explicitly say what was implied so clearly. I'd wanted to say no when he asked to see me after our official business, I'd wanted to shout it, storm out, and never see him again. But I couldn't do it. He held a terrible secret over me, and I couldn't bear to arbitrarily resist when I knew I'd bend if he pushed. I tried my best to push it from my mind and focus on work for the rest of the day.

By the time I got home, I was itching to burn off my excess energy and go for a run. When I walked through the door, Prince greeted me with the same unadulterated enthusiasm she always did, immediately easing my mind. I dropped down to one knee and she jumped into my arms, attacking my face with kisses. I scratched behind her floppy ears and ruffled her short, dark gray fur before I kissed the top of her head.

"Hey, sweet girl," I cooed. "Did you miss me?" I situated Prince back on the floor and gave her some pats from head to tail while I removed my messenger bag from my shoulder and toed out of my shoes. I started to tell Prince about my day—as I always did—while I walked toward my bedroom. She was my shadow, nails clicking on the laminate flooring.

I quickly changed into my running gear, talking away while Prince sat next to the bed, occasionally tilting her head while trying to understand my rambling. She really was the sweetest dog. She followed me back out to the front door where I grabbed her leash from the hook by the door. She sat for me without a command as I snapped it onto the O-ring on her collar. I gave her another pet on her head, then we were out the door.

We ran along the Lakefront Trail for an hour, taking in the views of the boats on the lake to one side and the cityscape on the other. Prince was ten years old, and impeccably healthy. She had no trouble on our nightly runs. It had been hard work for me in the beginning, but I grew to like the exertion over the years. Running gave me a chance to clear my mind and take in the beauty around me that I so easily overlooked. The sun warmed my skin, reminding me that I'd forgotten to wear sunscreen. The hotter days meant Prince would have to start wearing her boots again to protect her footpads. She hated them—and probably me—when I first put them on her a few years ago, but the adjustment period had been short.

I held her leash slack, not really needing it for her to obey, but using it anyway to abide by the regulations and keep other people at ease. Prince was a blue nose pit bull and because of that, some people were wary or frightened of her. It broke my heart to see people react that way, though there wasn't much I could do to convince them otherwise in passing. Keeping her leashed in off-leash areas was another precaution I took for her safety as well. If it was late and no one else was around, I'd unclip the leash and let her tear around or we'd play fetch. Fetch often ended in me watching her eat sticks.

Back at home, I unclipped Prince, refreshed her water bowl, and scooped out her dinner while she patiently waited. She always looked like she was smiling, but that was especially true when food was involved. I set her dish down and gave the command for her to know it was okay to move and devour her high-protein kibble. Satisfied that she was looked after, I turned around in my small kitchen and flipped on the back burner. Baked chicken breast and a rice pilaf sounded like a pretty decent idea for dinner. It was my favorite thing to make, and I'd hoped it would let me hang on to the peace I'd achieved from my run just a bit longer. I'd have plenty of time to worry about Bryan Rettger later.

I STOOD OUTSIDE of the building my GPS led me to. The storefront had large windows and painted white bricks that needed some freshening up. Double-checking the address once more, I sighed and opened the door to let myself in. Bryan was nowhere in sight, so I took a few moments to take in the space. It was dusty and full of rows of shelving, like it was once a bookstore or small convenience store. Given the location and dark paint on the walls, I'd say it was the former. The space extended further back into another room. The door to the room was propped open, but I couldn't see inside from where I stood. I figured Bryan had to be back there and called out for him. Footsteps caught my attention from beyond the door, quick and light, making me doubt it was in fact Bryan coming my way.

He was pretty solid looking and muscular. I'd have imagined him to be heavy-footed. And I was wrong. Bryan pushed the door open and smiled when he saw me. He had on a white zip-up suit, likely to protect his clothes, and kind of looked like a jovial serial killer. Or maybe that was just how I saw him, given the circumstances. He didn't look like a sleazy asshole, what with his easy smile and soft green eyes, but here we were. As he approached, I noticed that he had subtle dimples under the scruff covering his jaw and lip, the same intense black as the hair on his head. There were white chunks of what looked like plaster in his hair, which would explain the serial killer get-up.

"Hey," he greeted, speaking in a soft tone incongruous with his rugged brand of handsome, as Eve had described it. Then again, him opening a bakery of all things seemed pretty out of character as well.

"Good morning," I returned, hating how stiff I sounded. Bryan's furrowed brow showed me that he'd noticed as well, which only made the rest of my body go tense. He took another step toward me and I reflexively stepped back, bumping into the corner of one of the shelves.

Bryan froze mid-step and held out his hands palms up. "Hey, hey, what's wrong?"

I felt lightheaded. What would I do if he told me he wanted... God, I couldn't even finish the thought without feeling bile rise in my throat.

"Elijah, are you okay? You don't look so hot." Bryan looked around the room and nodded over at a chair near the wall. I sat down and couldn't meet his eyes when he knelt in front of me.

"I'm good." I nodded then added, "Just a bit tired. So, this is the space, huh?"

Bryan cocked his head to the side, clearly not buying my reasoning for my behavior, but he let it slide. "Yeah. This is my baby. It's not much to look at right now," he said as he gestured around, "but we'll get there. Can I get you some water or something?"

"No, thank you. I'm really okay. How about you show me around, so I can get to planning." Bryan still didn't look convinced, though he nodded and proceeded to do just that for the next hour.

We looked at the inside space where Bryan showed me design plans, and we walked a couple of blocks to see what else was around and what kind of foot traffic there was during lunchtime. I had some pretty decent notes by the time we returned to the store and was eager to get started on a plan. The uneasiness I felt earlier was pushed to the back of my mind while we were out, but now that we were alone again I could feel it creeping back.

Bryan was a really nice guy, and under different circumstances, we maybe could have been friends, even. The whole blackmail thing was kind of a big deal, and something I couldn't ignore no matter how much I tried.

"So, what do you think?" he asked, snapping me back to reality. "You look like you're thinking."

"Ah, the space has a lot of potential and the location is great. You have a lot of work to do, but the designs you showed me will help me tailor the marketing strategy. I want it to be harmonious with the way you're going to conduct business and the vibe this place will have. I need to do a lot of research, but I can make a campaign that'll be appropriate for what you hope to convey."

Bryan smiled at me and stepped closer—close enough so

that I could see his dimples again. "I totally made the right call with you."

His pale green eyes turned dark and pinned me in a way that made me want to run. I thought he was going to kiss me before he glanced off to the side and returned a neutral gaze on me. He asked me if I'd like to accompany him for a drink to celebrate our new working relationship, and I couldn't stand the waiting any longer.

"What do you want from me?" I murmured. It felt like that was all I knew how to ask him.

"Ah, I'm not sure what you mean." He sounded genuinely confused.

"Just tell me what you want me to do. I'll do it. I'll do anything if it means you won't tell anyone about…" My eyes shot to my feet as my voice trailed off. I managed to speak without wavering, but now that it was out, I wanted to crawl inside myself and hide. Or throw up.

"What? Elijah, Jesus Christ—do you think I'm trying to blackmail you or something?" Bryan sounded stricken, like the words tasted off on his tongue.

I chanced a glance up at him, startled by his tone more than his words. He looked just as troubled as his voice had suggested. And then I felt like the biggest idiot, and an asshole. Shame and embarrassment battled within me for dominance, and I turned away so Bryan couldn't see my expression, as if that would make the situation better. Heat flooded my cheeks and my pulse was pounding so hard that I started to sweat.

"Is that why you've been acting weird around me? I figured you were a little spooked, but damn. I'm really sorry if I said anything to imply… what you thought I was imply-ing. I swear, that thought never crossed my mind."

We stood in an awkward silence for what felt like ages. I kept my eyes glued to the floor while Bryan had taken a couple of steps back and tapped his foot—not in an impatient way, but more like a nervous tick.

"This is my fault," I mumbled. "You've been nothing but kind, yet I went ahead and let my paranoia take over, and I vilified you in my mind. That wasn't fair." I shifted my eyes from the floor to Bryan's face, relieved he wasn't angry with me. He had every right to be considering I'd assumed he was the worst.

He shook his head lightly. "It's not anyone's fault, man. We have a unique history. I get why you'd be more on guard—"

"And leap to worst-case conclusions? Yeah. I'm not the most socially adept person, if I hadn't already made that painfully clear." I pounded my fists on top of one another in front of me, suddenly feeling like I had to do something with my hands. Self-deprecation was nothing new to me, but I generally didn't verbalize it in front of other people. Then again, I didn't usually talk to other people *to* verbalize it.

Bryan cracked a small half smile and shrugged his shoulders once. The silence between us felt lighter than it had moments ago. Bryan broke it the second time.

"My offer for a drink still stands, you know. No pressure."

The urge to say no was still strong within me. Bryan might not be the sleazy asshole my mind had painted him to be, but we still shared a unique past that frankly made me uncomfortable. I was relieved to know he wouldn't tell anyone, but just knowing that he *knew* made me want to reject his request and go home. However, I had a job to do. Spending time with Bryan under different circumstances didn't seem like it would be a hardship, so I would do my job and I would try. I owed him at least that.

"Yeah," I started, "let's go get a drink. The first round is on me for being an idiot."

Bryan's face lit up, and he laughed. "You're not an idiot, but I'm not going to turn down a free drink."

Well, at least he was easy to please.

WE WALKED over to a bar that we'd passed by earlier. It had air-conditioning and it wasn't very busy, so I was instantly a fan. The place was very… woody, for lack of a better term— on the verge of being a dive bar. Wood-paneled walls, scuffed-up wooden floors, wooden chairs and tables… woody. It was clean, just old and lacking the flair of newer sports bars.

Bryan had led us over to a corner table, away from the TVs and other patrons, and we were greeted by a server way sooner than I'd expected. She came back a few minutes later with two open bottles of pilsner. She set them on the wooden table in front of us, gave a smile and some kind words then moved on to serve another table, leaving us to fill the conversational void in her wake.

"So…" Bryan said experimentally. "Do you want to just jump right in?"

I took a deep breath and nodded before reaching for my beer.

Bryan ran his fingers through his black hair, pushing it back from his forehead. "I'll start. I lost a bet when I was twenty that resulted in me doing one porn shoot. I kind of liked it, and the money was really good, so I did several more videos." He took a long drink and rolled his shoulders, his fingers never leaving the bottle. "It was my first time having my own money and doing something for me. The fact that it was kind of taboo just made it more alluring."

I scrunched up my nose at that. From what I read in his

file, the Rettgers were a rather wealthy family—Bryan didn't need to make money from porn.

"I know what you're thinking," he said with a smirk. "Why does someone from a well-off family need to do porn for extra cash?"

"Am I so transparent?" I deadpanned.

"Kind of. It's also a fair question. My parents would have given me the money had I asked for it. I have no doubts about that. See, university was the first time I ever left Texas. I grew up working the ranch, like all of my brothers, so I never had a normal job."

"Um, porn isn't what I'd consider a normal job," I said dryly. Bryan's laughter spilled out of him, surprising me. I've been told by too many people that I was a bit abrasive, though Bryan didn't seem bothered by my shitty personality.

"No. It gave me financial independence for the first time in my life. After that, I took on a part-time job—one where I got to keep my clothes on."

I snorted at that. "Where did you get Rhett Ryder from?"

Bryan's eyebrows jumped up at that. "Oh. You remember."

"I—um… yes, I remember," I replied quietly.

"Rhett is a nickname from my varsity baseball days, taken from my last name. There was already a Brian on the team and it was confusing. Ryder is my mom's maiden name. I thought it sounded pretty porny." He took another drink then tilted the bottle in my direction before he set it down. "Why didn't you use a fake name?"

A humorless laugh rushed out of me, the robust quality of it shocking me. "I—uh, I didn't really know what I was doing. Looking back, my name was pretty worthless, so it didn't really matter."

"What makes you say that?"

"I didn't have anything or anyone. If news of what I've

done came out now, that would be different, but I had nothing back then." The words came out a little faster than they normally did. I reached for my beer to shut myself up before I said too much.

"What about your dog?" Bryan asked.

"Excuse me?" How did he know about Prince?

"You said you had a sick puppy and needed money for her. I don't remember what you said her name was, though." Bryan's forehead was wrinkled, like he was deep in thought. "I was looking forward to meeting her after the shoot."

"Oh. Yes. Her name is Prince."

"Like, 'Purple Rain'?"

"No, Princess Leia," I said fondly. I had the sudden urge to tell him all about her, but I'd been told before by exes that I talked about her too much. I changed the subject instead. "Although I do really like Prince's music too."

"*Star Wars*, right?" Bryan asked with his head slightly cocked.

Was he being serious? "Yes, it's from *Star Wars*. Have… have you *not* seen any of the *Star Wars* movies?" I asked disbelievingly. He couldn't be serious.

Bryan shrugged guiltily. "I've seen some of the one with Liam Neeson. It was"—he paused, waving his free hand in the air in front of him—"interesting."

Oh my God. I was wrong about us maybe being able to be friends. So, so wrong. Who in their right mind hadn't seen at least one entry in the best franchise of all time? My fingers tightened around the bottle in my hand, cool condensation dripping over my fingers. I cringed both at my hyperbole and at Bryan's tragic admission.

"Oh, Jesus. You're looking at me like I've just committed a sacrilegious offense," Bryan teased.

I tipped my hand back and forth in a so-so manner. "You

kind of have. I don't want to sound like an elitist asshole, but I find what you just told me to be rather troubling."

"You're not the only one. I've gotten shit about it for years from my roommate. He goes to see all the new ones and tries to get me to go, but sci-fi has never been my thing. Shit, I'm not making this any better." He laughed again and flashed me an apologetic look. "I'll watch them all, how about that?"

"I can't force you to do anything, though I suppose I can judge you about it if you don't."

He smiled, all white teeth and dimples. "Does that mean you're going to stay on with my bakery?"

"Yes. I said I would. Especially now that I know you're not a blackmailer and just a guy with tragic taste in cinema." God, was I actually teasing him?

"Ouch. Okay. I promise I'll watch them. Eventually."

"You can borrow them, if you'd like. I have the series on Blu-ray." Lending out my things to others wasn't something I normally did—whether by choice or because there wasn't anyone to share with was debatable.

"I appreciate the offer, but I don't actually have a Blu-ray player. Mac has an Xbox in his room, which isn't always convenient. I guess I could buy one."

I chewed on my bottom lip and studied Bryan. He *was* a nice guy. Even back then... he was kind to me. I could return that kindness now, like normally functioning, well-adjusted people did. "We can watch them at my place, if you want."

His eyes opened wide. In surprise? Shock? Probably both. "Like, movie night?" he asked.

I nodded. "I guess you could call it that. Really, it would be my charitable contribution to society. Sorry. That was rude."

Bryan laughed again and shook his head. "Nah, don't

apologize. I like your brand of humor. We'll see if you're right, though."

We both finished our beers and ordered another round when the server came back. I wasn't planning on staying for a second, but it was nice—albeit still mildly strange—talking to someone else other than Eve or Prince.

"You mentioned Mac before. Is he your roommate?" I was pretty sure he was; I just wanted to talk to him more.

"That's right. He's also the guy I lost that bet to back in university. Cheeky fucker." There was tenderness in his voice that told me he really cared about Mac. That, and the fact that they'd been friends for so long, especially after a bet like that.

"Why on earth did he make you do gay porn? That just seems like another layer to your punishment."

Bryan cocked an eyebrow at me and said, "Well, I'm gay, so doing straight porn probably would have been very difficult for me."

Foot, meet mouth. I blanched. I fumbled my hands on the table, but there wasn't a new bottle for me to hide behind. Bryan never took his eyes off me, which only made me fidget more. "I'm sorry. I didn't mean to suggest any—"

Bryan's hand shot up, silencing me. "It's okay, Elijah. Does me being gay make you uncomfortable?"

I shook my head immediately. "No. The shit that falls out of my mouth is the only thing making me uncomfortable. I'm not, if you were wondering."

"Not what?"

"Gay," I said quickly, causing me to visibly cringe.

Bryan chuckled at me as the server returned with our new beers. I took mine as soon as she set it down and drank half of it in one go. "We're going to need another round, please," Bryan said to the waitress.

"Of course," she said before leaving us again.

Still grinning at me, Bryan lifted his bottle to his lips and swallowed down just as much as I had. "I didn't think you were gay. Not after your reaction to my admission. I'd assumed you were when we first met, but given the circumstances, that was an honest mistake."

"I'm really not offended. It's just... nothing I say today is coming out right."

"Maybe you're just out of practice."

"I'm not used to other people. Not like this." As if *that* explained anything to him.

"I'm going to give you another out. You made your offer before you knew about me, and I won't hold it against you. I don't want to make you uncomfortable."

I really considered his words this time instead of answering immediately. I never knew any gay people, and I really didn't have an aversion to them either. Bryan was still the exact same guy whose company I was enjoying enough to invite over to my apartment. It was actually kind of a relief that we wouldn't be talking about women—I didn't need to be reminded of my failed relationships or shortcomings as a lover. I took another drink and looked Bryan in the eye, for what felt like the first time in ages.

"Which evening would you like to come over? I was thinking we'd start with the original trilogy so you can see how *Star Wars* is supposed to be before we watch the prequels. The newer films are an improvement from the prequels, but the original trilogy is still the gold standard."

A smiled spread across Bryan's face and he bowed his head at me. "Your problem must be over; what you said just now sounded like it came out right to me."

"Yeah, I guess it did."

FOUR

BRYAN

"WE ALREADY TALKED ABOUT THIS last night, dude."

"I know, I know," I said, holding my phone to my ear and pacing around the front space of my soon-to-be bakery. "Just let me be happy for a sec."

Mac sighed, and I could just picture him sprawled out upside down on the couch in his damn underwear. He insisted it helped him articulate his thoughts better when he was on the phone, but I thought he just enjoyed being a weirdo.

"That's fine, Bry. I want you to be happy, but Elijah isn't gay."

"I know that." I sounded petulant, even to my own ears.

"We don't need another repeat of senior year, when you were crushing on that third-baseman from Joliet. Oh, wait, we already got a repeat. Thrice! Don't make this a fourth."

Mac had a point, even if I hated to admit it. My track record with straight men wasn't great. "Does it really count if I already had the crush from way back, though?"

Mac scoffed. I heard some rustling and could imagine

him sliding all over the couch. "Zip it. What're you making me for dinner?"

I was about to give him some options when the door to the shop opened, the sun streaking through the overly dusty air. The guys I'd been expecting to come clear away the shelves and trash walked inside in work boots, thick gloves, and dark blue coveralls, looking every bit the sexy blue-collar type. I pushed that thought from my mind and waved my free hand at them in greeting.

"Ah, that's a surprise," I said to Mac. "I've got to go. The guys are here."

"Love you," Mac drawled.

"See you later."

"Wait, say it ba—"

I disconnected the call with Mac whining in my ear then smiled at the group of men standing before me, awaiting instruction. I introduced myself to each of them before setting them about their tasks. While they cleared out the front, I made my way to the back, picked up a crowbar, and went to work ripping down some wall-mounted shelves.

WE WERE TRAILING the opposing team by two points in the bottom of the ninth inning. Our opponents were a team of firefighters, and they beat us last month. The game's just for fun and really shouldn't have been taken seriously, but as former all-star varsity players, Mac and I took that shit very seriously and we were determined not to give them another victory. I was up to bat with Mac on first, and our buddy Axel was on third, ready to bolt for the home plate.

No pressure, right?

I cracked my neck and stepped up to the plate, rotating the bat in my hand and firming up my grip on the wooden handle. The pitcher was that same smug bastard who struck Mac out last game. Mac made it out to be some big battle-of-the-blonds drama and wanted redemption. Unfortunately, he didn't get that chance. The pitcher intentionally threw for shit and walked Mac to the open first base. It was a smart move strategically, and I couldn't knock the man for it. Mac had too much to prove, and they were playing to win.

I was a known power-hitter, so I was sure to expect some tricky shit coming my way. No matter what happened, I had to connect. And hard. I rolled my shoulders then spread my feet wide, dropped my hips, and shifted my weight to the balls of my feet. Raising the bat up and over my right shoulder, I kept my eyes on the pitcher after winking at Mac. My breaths came in steady to keep the tension out of my stance and my attention sharp. Smug blondie up on the mound grinned then whipped off a curve ball toward the inside. I swung for it and didn't connect, but instantly went back into my batting stance. One was nothing. I had two more shots to nail the fucker.

The pitcher nodded, presumably at the catcher, wound up, and released the ball with a snap of his wrist, just like last time. But not quite. Not thinking he'd give me the same pitch twice, I took a chance and adjusted my swing for an outside curveball. I swung with every bit of strength I had, and when the loud crack of the bat hitting the ball reached my ears, I knew the game was over. The force of the hit sent a familiar jolt up my forearms, bringing a smile to my face. I watched as the ball sailed high over the first-baseman, ultimately hitting the fence deep in the right field. I tipped my helmet to the pitcher, dropped my bat, and leisurely jogged around the bases. Mac was waiting for me at the home plate and gave me a bear hug, complete with a couple of back slaps.

"I could kiss you, you hunky motherfucker," he yelled with a wide smile.

I burst out laughing, as did several of our teammates. "Maybe we'll skip that and you can buy the first round instead," I offered, getting the approving cheers of several of the guys.

"Fuck it—done!" Mac hugged me a second time then Axel jumped onto my back, his legs wrapping around me tight. Axel was just twenty-one and the youngest—and smallest—guy on our team. What he lacked in size and strength, he made up for with speed and accuracy. He was our reliable contact-hitter and a very valuable member of the team.

"All right, Axe-Man, get the hell off me before I throw out my back."

"That was so freakin' cool, man," Axel shouted, his voice kicked up higher than usual due to his excitement. He slid off my back and seemed to vibrate on the ground. "Did you see the look on that *pendejo's* face? Amazing."

Several more colorful words were exchanged between several guys before we lined up and shook hands with the other team. Because, you know, good sportsmanship and all that. The guys with kids and significant others went home, but Mac, Axel, a new guy named Santiago, and Maxim all went out for a few celebratory rounds. A few turned into too many, as it often did, and I was in a world of hurt by the time my head hit my pillow. Messy, overindulgent nights meant putting in double the work at the gym the next day. I wasn't looking forward to that.

I KNOCKED TWICE on Elijah's door as I took deep breaths and willed myself to relax. I wasn't the guy who let his nerves control him, but Elijah brought it out in me. I kept replaying Mac's words in my head and tried my best to remind myself not to get too attached, but if I was honest with myself, it was probably going to be a losing battle.

The door opened to those beautiful, rich brown eyes and a tentative smile. "Hi," Elijah said, voice matching his smile.

"Hi," I echoed. I refrained from telling him how hot he looked in the white tee and blue basketball shorts he wore. The two times I'd seen him prior he was looking pretty spiffy and put together. Standing in the doorway in front of me, he looked relaxed—his clothing did, anyway. He looked hot in his work clothes too, in a different way. When I saw him all buttoned up I wanted to mess him up and make him pant. Seeing him all casual… yeah, all right, I still wanted to mess him up and get him all hot and sweaty, but I liked seeing a new side of him.

He made no sign of letting me inside, so I held up the canvas bag I was holding and grinned. "I brought some snacks for the movie. I wasn't sure what you liked, so there's probably too much."

"Oh, shit. I'm sorry. Come inside." He stepped aside, clearing the way for me.

The moment I passed the threshold, I was assaulted by paws on my legs and the cutest little gray furbaby-face looking up at me. How I'd forgotten in the last few days that he had a dog was beyond me. Her tail was wagging like crazy and it looked like she was smiling at me. I held my breath so I wouldn't gasp in delight, set my bag down, and let her sniff and lick my hand before I rubbed her cheeks and behind her ears.

"*Oooh my God.*" She—Prince, right?—licked my face with even more enthusiasm now that I was down on her level. I heard the door close behind me, and Elijah circled around to stand in front of me and tried to call her back. She disregarded the command and rolled over so I could rub her cute little belly.

"I'm sorry she jumped on you. She gets really excited with new people. I can put her in my bedroom if you want."

I shook my head and scratched under her chin while she licked my palm. "No need to apologize. She's beautiful. Besides"—I turned my attention to Prince and matched the grin she gave me—"this is your house. Yeah, it is." I looked back up at Elijah to see him smiling down at me. Or Prince. He was probably smiling at his dog and it was just wishful thinking on my part. "Is she a pit bull?"

He nodded his head and rubbed his hands in front of him, like he wasn't sure what to do with them. "She's a blue nose pit bull. I don't have papers for her or anything, but she's healthy and happy."

"I can see that. Gosh, I bet you were one cute little puppy back in the day." It slipped out before I could think not to say it. My eyes shot up in time to see Elijah's smile had faltered and he'd crossed his arms over his chest. Right—no more inadvertently bringing up the past.

I gave Prince's belly one more rub before I stood up and asked where I could put the bag of snacks. Elijah rubbed the back of his neck and pointed over his shoulder to the right. I looked around him and saw a cream-colored granite island off to the right where the kitchen must have been. We made our way toward it and the rest of the kitchen came into view, displaying dark brown cabinetry and stainless-steel appliances. The island was huge, doubling as extra counter space and for entertaining, based on its location. Beyond the kitchen near large windows was the living room, adorned with a comfortable-looking brown suede couch, a rectangular glass table in front of it, and a small black TV stand with a bigger than what I was expecting TV on it—maybe sixty inches. I set my bag down on the island, and upon closer inspection of the space, I saw some mounted surround-sound speakers.

So he really likes movies. Noted.

"This place is really nice. I like the open concept. Did you move in recently?" It was neat and uncluttered, but almost to the point where personal effects hadn't been unpacked. I saw no photos of family or anything he liked decorating the space.

"Thank you," Elijah replied. "But no. I've lived here for a couple years now. I know it's pretty... plain, but it suits me."

Did he think he was plain? I wanted to ask what he meant by that, but it didn't seem like something he really wanted to delve into, so I changed gears. "Well, I like it. I'm used to things being clean; Mac sucks in the kitchen, but he cleans the rest of our place when he needs a break from working."

"Sounds like the ideal roommate."

"Well, I'm not messy *and* I cook, so I think I'm the catch between the two of us."

Elijah smirked at me and relaxed a bit more. His arms were crossed again, though he looked more at ease and less defensive. "I'll give you that. I've lived alone for a long time and am not as talented in the kitchen as I probably should be. Speaking of, it's fairly obvious, but here's the kitchen." He motioned to the fridge, oven, and microwave against the wall. "The bathroom is right behind you. It's the door on the left."

"And if I go for the door on the right?" I asked playfully.

"You might end up having to buy me a new washer and dryer," Elijah deadpanned.

I snorted a laugh and clenched my teeth to hold back the huge toothy smile that threatened to break out on my face. It wasn't that it was the funniest joke I'd ever heard, I was just happy that Elijah was joking with me at all. Sober. At least I thought he was sober.

From where we stood I saw another door behind the couch. Process of elimination told me it was his bedroom, all other doors either having been explained or obviously closets. The door to his room was closed, and I couldn't help but wonder what it looked like inside. Would he have pictures in there? Maybe something else personal? *No shit, it's personal. The door is closed.*

I pushed the line of thought from my mind and let my eyes fall on Prince where she sat at Elijah's feet before I made eye contact with the man. "So, I'm really excited, but also pretty nervous."

His eyebrows drew together and his head cocked ever so slightly to the side. "*You're* nervous? Why?"

"The hype surrounding these movies is too damn big, man. There's a lot of pressure to like them or face even more public shame than I do for having not already seen them." I was only half serious, of course, but I made Elijah laugh, which I already knew he didn't do enough.

"I promise I won't judge you for not liking the movies. However, I *will* continue to judge you until you've seen them."

"We'd better get started then."

Elijah told me what drinks were in the fridge and asked me if I wanted anything. I settled on a can of blood orange San Pellegrino, we popped some popcorn, and headed over to the couch. I realized I'd forgotten a snack in my bag and doubled back to the island to grab a bag of chocolate-covered almonds before making my way back into the living room.

With a bowl of freshly popped popcorn in hand, I sat down on the opposite end of the couch, giving Elijah ample space. Prince was curled up around his feet, seemingly finished lavishing me in attention. For now. I'd win her back after the movie.

Elijah asked me if I was ready, his tone tight and unsure. I could see the tension in the way he held his body, and it made me bite back a smile. I didn't think he was nervous about being alone with me because of our past or that I was gay; I thought he was on edge over having someone else here, in his private space—who that person was didn't really matter. It was his idea, yes, but it seemed spur of the moment. Elijah said he wasn't very socially adept, and he was nervous having a drink out in public with me, so the rest was just an educated guess on my part.

I gave him an easy thumbs-up and said I was good to go. He hit play and the instantly recognizable score filled the room, followed by scrolling text on the screen. "Episode Four —shouldn't we start with Episode One? Is there an Episode One?"

Elijah sighed and hit pause. He explained to me that Episodes one through three came out between nineteen ninety-nine and two thousand and five, but take place before the events of A New Hope, which came out in nineteen seventy-seven. When I understood, he hit play, gave Prince a rub behind an ear, and settled back against the couch.

Oh, reading… a lot of reading.

I stole a peek over at Elijah—he was completely enamored. His eyes were wide and attentive, darting back and forth, taking in all the words rolling by. He had the beginnings of a soft smile pulling at his lips and was so into this and so damn cute. It would be rude not to take this seriously. I turned my attention back to the TV and dug into the popcorn.

The movie ended, but instead of turning it off, Elijah turned the volume down a few notches then turned to me.

"Well? What did you think?" He'd relaxed once the movie was on, but now that it was over and his expectant brown eyes were on me, the tension was back in his lean body.

"Overall I really liked it," I started. "Honestly, it didn't feel like I was watching a movie from the seventies at all once I got sucked in. I don't usually like classics, but I was pleasantly surprised."

Elijah's shoulders dropped back to a relaxed state, and I saw his chest deflate when he released the breath he'd been holding. "Really? You liked it?" His voice took on a hopeful edge.

I smiled and nodded. "Yeah. I mean, the 'Evil Galactic Empire' bit from the prologue was a little cheesy, but I tried not to judge and watched with an open mind. Vader was pretty cool—he's so mysterious. Oh! And why are his powers so much stronger than the old guy's? Obi... the old white-haired guy." I tried to remember all the names, but there were so many characters and places and ships and... everything.

"Ben. Obi-Wan Kenobi. I'd love to tell you why, but I can't without spoiling way too much." The corners of his lips lifted ever so slightly, and the tips of his ears flushed. "I'd love to discuss it with you more once you've seen the rest of the movies."

Prince had jumped up on the couch halfway through the movie and rested her head on Elijah's knee. He patted her until she'd fallen asleep again, but she'd woken up near the end of the movie. She stayed next to Elijah, staying in constant contact with him at all times. The pair of them were really something.

"I can see why you like Leia," I said, gently stroking Prince's back. "She's strong, feisty, and doesn't take any bullshit from anyone."

Elijah nodded. "She's amazing, especially for when this came out. When I found Prince years ago she was underweight and sick. I didn't know what to do with her. After I'd had her for a couple days, I knew I couldn't give her up. I named her after the strongest heroine I knew." He spoke so fondly, petting Prince the whole time.

"She's lucky to have you."

He shook his head and smiled weakly at me. "It's the other way around, really. She saved me."

I wanted to ask what he meant by that, though I thought I already knew. Loneliness, perhaps. He seemed content enough not having a lot of friends, and I'd bet that that had to do with how much he loved his dog. It was sweet, but it also made my chest ache. Elijah was too damn young to be as jaded as I thought he was.

"You're both lucky." I looked over at Elijah and saw he had his attention on what must have been a particularly interesting series of folds in his shirt. "R2-D2 is irrationally adorable. Why is a robot so damn cute?"

Light flooded back into Elijah's eyes, and his head rolled back against the couch. "Isn't he, though? They gave a speechless droid so much life with just a series of beeps."

"He's kinda sassy. I dig it. The gold one is funny too. And Han... Young Harrison Ford was way too sexy. He had so much swagger." I was deliberately holding back on the comment about Ford, planning on not saying it at all. I decided I'd trust when Elijah said my homosexuality wasn't an issue for him and speak candidly, like I would with any of my other friends—okay, maybe not *quite* as candidly. Not yet, anyway.

My comments about Ford didn't faze him in the least. He laughed and nodded, stating that Han was a really cool guy and someone he'd always admired. We both agreed that Luke started out too whiny, but he promised me that he got better by the next movie.

"Are we going to watch that one too? Not necessarily today in case you're busy, but, like, eventually?" *Smooth.*

"Yeah, if you want to keep watching them, we can arrange another evening. I can't do it today, though. I have to take Prince for a run soon." He sounded almost apologetic, which was silly.

"That's okay. Once we check our schedules we can pick another time." I added a grin to show that there were no hard feelings about us not continuing today, but more so it was because he'd effectively told me it was time to leave, and I didn't even think he realized he'd done it.

I stood up, followed almost immediately by Elijah and Prince. Her tail was going crazy, and she ran to the front door and sat down. I guess she knew it was time for that run as well. "Do you go running with her every day?"

"Yes. We go for a walk or light jog in the morning and a run along the Lakefront Trail in the evening. I feel bad about her being home all day and like to see that she gets plenty of activity."

"You're a good dog-dad, Elijah." I knelt down to pet Prince once more, and she showered me in eager kisses again.

"Eli." I looked up at Elijah, momentarily startled by his voice. "You can call me Eli. And thanks."

Eli. Yes! I managed to maintain my composure as he clipped on Prince's leash and rode the elevator down to the lobby with me. I ordered an Uber in the elevator, and he waited with me for the car to come. We talked more about the movie for a few minutes until a blue Fusion pulled up and I got an alert that my ride had arrived. We said a quick goodbye, and I got in the car. As it pulled away, I turned back and watched Eli and Prince jog off toward the lake. Yeah, it was too damn late to not get attached.

FIVE

ELI

I'D BEEN RESTLESS AT WORK ALL MORNING. My concentration was nonexistent, which was very uncharacteristic of me. Eve had to have noticed, but she didn't comment. I'd been feeling this way since Bryan went home after the movie last week. Having someone in my space wasn't half the nightmare that I was expecting it to be, and I'd even managed to have fun once I relaxed. Bryan said he wanted to continue with the franchise, but we hadn't set a night.

I was a coward and was waiting for Bryan to text me first. I didn't want to seem like a desperate weirdo, even if that was what I was. I hadn't had a male friend since university. Samir was exempt since I wouldn't know him without Eve. The two of us have never hung out without her. Bryan was an unexpected chance for something new. For whatever reason, he seemed to really like my company, and I didn't want to mess that up by being overbearing.

That was the plan, at least. As I sat at my desk and alternated between shuffling around the same stack of papers and scrolling through depressing news articles, the plan fell to pieces and I pulled up Bryan's cell number. I dialed out using my work phone figuring I could use the pretense of a work question to mask my true intent.

He picked up on the third ring.

"Hello?"

"Hey, good morning. It's Eli. Harper, in case you know more than one guy named Eli." I cringed at myself in silence, looking up to see Eve watching me with a raised eyebrow. I'd deal with her later.

"Oh, hey." His voice changed; it softened, maybe. "What's up?"

I heard banging in the background as well as a few muffled voices. "I had a question about the bakery, but if now is a bad time, I can call back later."

"No, no, now is fine. Just let me step into another room." Footsteps took prominence in my ear as the voices and banging quieted. "Is this better?"

Oh. He moved for my consideration? "Yes, that's great." Unsure of what else to say now that he was actually on the line, I chewed my thumbnail and doodled on the edge of a paper in front of me.

"Are you still with me, Eli?" Bryan asked. He sounded like he was smiling. Oddly enough, I could easily picture it— did dimples always stand out to me?

"Ah, shit. Yes, sorry."

"Busy day?"

"Yes." I lied. It wasn't like I could tell him I was stressed about potentially fucking up our budding friendship. Jesus Christ, I was pathetic.

"I won't keep you then. What was your question?"

"My ques—right." I'd completely forgotten about that. "It was regarding the… color scheme for the seating area. I don't seem to have any notes for that."

Bryan proceeded to tell me his plan for white-ash-stained

tables, textures, off-white paint on all walls except for the restored brick one, and splashes of bold colors with fresh flowers and accents. I paused again when he finished explaining his vision for the space, trying to work myself up for the actual reason for my call.

"Thank you for filling in the gaps. I had another question as well."

"Yeah, fire away."

"Do you want to watch the next movie this week? *Star Wars*, I mean." Because we were watching *so* many other movies together. "It's all right if you're busy." I hated that I sounded like an insecure teen girl asking the popular guy to prom.

"Absolutely," Bryan replied immediately and enthusiastically. "I can do any night this week except Saturday."

Relief washed over me in a crashing wave. "How about Friday? Is seven too late?"

"Nah, seven is perfect."

That would give me enough time to take Prince out for a run so I wouldn't have to shoo Bryan immediately out like I did last week. I thought about that after and felt shitty about it, despite not having noticed how it appeared at the time. Utterly relieved that Bryan wasn't mad at me, we said our goodbyes and I ended the call. As soon as the handset was back in its cradle, I groaned and banged my forehead against my desk, letting it sit there while I wallowed.

"I've kept my nose out of whatever's going on with ya this morning, but that ends now. What the bloody fuck was that call?" Eve. I should have waited until she'd left to call Bryan.

I groaned and lifted my head. "Was it as bad as it sounded to me?"

"It was awful, pet. Who were you talking to anyway?"

"Bryan," I mumbled. Eve cocked an eyebrow at me and I elaborated. "Bryan Rettger."

"You're watching flicks with your new client? I thought we were going to hate him—you were pretty tense last week after you met him. And at any subsequent mention of him for the first few days."

Great. I hadn't hidden that as well as I'd thought. "I got over what was bothering me. It was really just an epic misunderstanding. Bryan is a nice guy." I explained how we agreed to watch *Star Wars* at my apartment—leaving out the more complicated details—and that I thought I had a shot at being friends with him. Eve understood more than anyone what that meant to me.

"So," Eve started, "that holy show of a call was you being nervous about making a new friend? Oh, Eli," she crooned.

"No!" I spoke too soon. I sounded way too defensive to be believable. "No. I needed some details about the interior."

"*Ráiméis.*"

I'd come to know that as the Gaeilge version of "bull-shit." Of course Eve would see through that excuse.

"You have that information in that file on your desk. And I'll bet you have it in your handwritten notes too. It's okay to be anxious, but I think you can relax a bit. It sounds like the two of ye hit it off. Although it is a bit alarming that he hasn't seen those flicks."

Still in denial mode, I panicked and foolishly tried to defend my actions. "His vision for the bakery is really fresh, and I—"

"Shut your gob. Was that an intentional pun? Because it was almost as awful as that call. I'm calling bullshit on you, Elijah Harper."

She full-named me. I supposed the jig was up. "Fine. I called because I wanted to hang out again. But now I wish I hadn't. I was, well, me—weird and awkward, and now he's probably thinking I'm those things too."

"Stop with that. You're a good man. And the fact that you're pursing a new friendship at all speaks to how much you've grown since I've known you. Especially with a man."

I shot her a narrowed gaze, which didn't faze her in the slightest.

"Oh, please. Don't think for a second that I haven't noticed that you tend to get along with our female colleagues more than their male counterparts. You were cautious around Samir at first as well."

She had me there. I felt highly insecure around men, especially around alpha, macho guys. I'd always felt like more of an outsider, but that only worsened after I lost my mom and *did* truly become an outsider. "I just don't have a lot in common with a lot of guys," I said quietly, eyeing the room to make sure none of our colleagues were inadvertently privy to our conversation. "I don't really fit in."

A sympathetic smile graced Eve's face, but I couldn't maintain eye contact with her without feeling too exposed. "You're not so different, Eli. Not nearly as much as you think."

"Can… can we talk about this another time?" I stood up, gathering up some files and stuffing them in my messenger bag. I had an appointment at one and it was just barely quarter after eleven, but I needed to leave before the conversation led me to have a full-on existential crisis at work.

"Where are you going?"

"I have a lunch meeting with Hana from Wagz."

An amused snort came from Eve's direction. "Oh, that cute dog-walker. I still maintain that she fancies you."

I shook my head and pulled the strap of the bag over my shoulder. "We're not having this conversation again. I'll be back before three."

Eve let out a disbelieving "mm-hmm" and waved me off with a two-finger salute. The truth was I knew Hana was interested in me, and I felt horrible for not wanting to reciprocate. She was a very attractive young woman, but I felt zero sexual desire for her—or anyone. I still got horny and stuff, though the feelings were always fleeting, and never in conjunction with any of my relationships. Shitty sex was always cited as one of the secondary reasons for my failed attempts at love, but I couldn't help it. Maybe I truly was broken in some way.

Whatever.

Dwelling on things I couldn't change was a waste of time and energy, and I had to save the latter if I was going to survive diplomatically dodging Hana's advances.

I LEFT work early Friday night to ensure I'd have enough time to take Prince for a long run. By the time we got home I had just over half an hour before Bryan would be arriving. I stripped off my sweaty running clothes, took a quick shower, and dressed in a new pair of dark blue shorts and a white tee. I fed Prince and refreshed her water bowl before I rummaged around my fridge for my own supper. With Bryan set to arrive any minute, I opted against cooking something and made a quick peanut butter and jelly sandwich. It wasn't enough to satiate me, but I'd survive until after the movie.

Three bites into my dinner, a knock came from the front door. Prince stopped eating, and her head perked up toward the door. After I walked past her, she followed me then sat on command while I opened the door. Bryan and I greeted each other, and he was inside with the door closed behind him before Prince unleashed on him. He sank down to his knees and then lay flat on his back, lavishing her in friendly pets and the standard baby talk that never failed to make grown men look like adorable children.

Adorable…did I just think Bryan was adorable? Whatever. Moving on.

"Jesus, you'd think I don't love her enough or something," I said, commenting on how wild Prince was going for Bryan.

He laughed and sat up, letting Prince stand on his thighs and lick his face. "Dogs tend to like me a lot. I'm not sure why, but I like them too, so it works out just fine."

"Well, if it becomes too much, just let me know. Do you mind if I go finish my supper?" I pointed over my shoulder with my thumb to indicate the plate I'd left on the island.

"Of course. We'll be fine, won't we?" he whisper-shouted at Prince. "Yeah, we'll be all right."

With a smile on my face I walked back to my half-eaten sandwich to finish the task at hand. Bryan finished up with Prince and was taking a seat across from me as I popped the last bite into my mouth. He set a small backpack on the counter and pulled out some movie snacks and… a pair of black-rimmed glasses.

"I didn't know you wore glasses," I blurted out. Of course I didn't fucking know; we practically just met a couple of weeks ago.

He grinned enough for his dimples to show and slid the glasses up the bridge of his straight nose. I wouldn't have pictured him as the glasses type before, but they sure suited him.

"Yeah, I usually wear contacts. I was gutting the bakery today, and I prefer my glasses for that."

"I like them," I said at the same time his stomach growled. Loudly. "Wow. Um, can I make you something to eat?"

"It's all right, you don't have to cook for me. I can order

something, if that's cool with you." Bryan placed a hand on his stomach and grinned sheepishly.

"I've got tons of food here. You don't have to spend on takeout."

Bryan mulled it over for a few moments then cocked his head in my direction. "Are you still hungry?"

I nodded.

"If you really don't mind, how about I whip us up something? I'm more than just a pâtissier."

"Is that appropriate? I don't want to make you work for free." Although I really did want to agree. I was capable enough but nowhere near a chef.

"It wouldn't be free; this is your food after all." He paused and smirked before adding, "And as for it being appropriate? I'm no naked chef, so I think we'll be good there."

I felt heat burn through my cheeks and ears before casting my eyes to the counter. I couldn't believe I'd walked into a joke like that, but my reaction to it was even worse. Joking and speaking nonchalantly about sex were never things I was able to do—the fact that I was so awful at the act was a joke enough.

"I shouldn't have said that. I'm sorry."

"You didn't say anything wrong," I countered.

Bryan hummed in amusement. "So you're just transfixed by the crumbs on that plate, then? I won't make any more sexually charged jokes. I don't want to make you feel uncomfortable in your own home." His tone became solemn in a way I didn't like. He was normally an easygoing, lighthearted guy in my experience. That all changed when I started saying stupid shit, like when I reacted to his admission that he was gay. I sincerely didn't have a problem with that, but my stupid brain and mouth didn't always know how to communicate effectively.

I forced myself to make eye contact with him. I wasn't

afraid to face him so much as I was afraid for him to see *me*. "My reaction has nothing to do with you being gay, and everything to do with my own intimacy issues." I hadn't planned on saying more than that, but Bryan's green eyes were so intently focused on me that I couldn't stop talking. "With anyone I've ever dated there were always complaints regarding intimacy of any sort—especially… sex. I could never really get into it and give my partners what they needed. I don't know if that's something you've ever experienced, but it makes you feel like shit. What kind of man can't satisfy his partner? Apparently the same kind who doesn't know how to love them either."

Jesus. I'd basically just admitted that I sucked in bed— way to get people to like you. I braced myself, tapping my fingers on the counter, while I waited to be laughed at and ridiculed. But it never came.

"I'm sorry you've had some terrible experiences. Sex isn't something everyone enjoys, you know. It doesn't mean there's anything wrong with you—it's just the way you are. And that's okay. We all have our issues, and I'm not going to judge you."

I looked up and saw that Bryan was dead serious. The urge to hide faded away when I realized he wasn't going to make fun of me, and I felt strangely light-headed. I swayed on my feet, catching myself on the counter before I realized big, strong hands were holding my wrists.

"Are you okay?" Bryan asked, not even trying to hide the concern in his voice or on his face.

Prince must have sensed something was wrong with me and ran around the island to my feet. She jumped up on my leg and pawed at my thigh until I pet her head a few times and said I was all right. I reassured Bryan of that fact too and tried to pull away from him. He loosened his hold on me but told me to trade places with him and sit. Before my ass hit the barstool, Bryan was in my fridge and already pulling out ingredients.

"I'm going to assume that you like everything in here since you bought it?" he asked.

"That would be a safe assumption."

He gathered up a package of chicken breasts, bell peppers, spinach, and mozzarella. "Where can I find your spices? And do you have any pasta or rice?"

I indicated to the appropriate cupboards and watched Bryan work. He looked so comfortable and, for the first time, I saw why the bakery was a good idea for him. If he did sweets half as good as he was making supper look, I had no doubts his venture would be a success.

After watching him wash and prep the veggies, he expertly sliced two breasts in half—nope, not all the way in half. "What are you making?"

"Stuffed chicken breasts and a savory rice pilaf," he replied with an easy smirk.

"Is that a joke? That's, like, my favorite thing to make. Except for the stuffed part. That sounds too complicated. But delicious."

"I promise it'll be good."

We made comfortable conversation while he finished prepping our food and popped it in the oven. He mentioned wanting to go to the store to pick up a bottle of wine, but we settled on the beer in my fridge. We talked about the bakery and *Star Wars*, thankfully staying clear of any more tough topics. By the time the timer on the stove went off, I was mildly dismayed about our conversation coming to an end. Talking to Bryan was easy, and he listened to me without prejudice. I felt like I'd known him for a lot longer than I had. And after taking a bite of the gorgeous food he plated up, it became clear that we had to do this again. And again.

"Holy shit. You're a good cook," I said after swallowing a bite of the most succulent chicken I'd ever tasted.

"Just good?" he teased.

"You already know you're great at it."

"Fact," he said with a smile. "I really enjoy cooking and baking for other people. I'm pretty lazy when it's just for me."

I eyed him up and down from where he sat next to me and scoffed. "I don't believe for a second that you're lazy with anything."

"Dude. Come over to my place on a Sunday afternoon and you'll see just how lazy I can get."

I knew it wasn't a real invitation, but I couldn't stop myself from being happy. Something as simple as going to a friend's house to hang out was something I hadn't done with another guy since high school. Eve invited me over occasionally, though she was more focused on getting me out and "socialized," as she'd put it. That socialization usually left me wanting nothing more than to go home and get in bed. If I was unlucky enough to get hit on, I had to endure getting-to-know-you small talk that was just a waste of time.

But isn't that what I'm doing with Bryan?

With Bryan it was different. I wasn't going to date him and then ruin it with my inadequacies. We weren't going to be *more*, and that made it a lot less daunting. I wanted to get to know Bryan. Not having the expectation of something more was liberating. Of course, I didn't have that with Eve either, but Bryan was my first guy friend—it felt different somehow.

"I wouldn't mind that sometime." My voice was low, yet that failed to mask any uncertainty bleeding through.

"For real? Any time you want to, just let me know. I'll make sure Mac is decent." The look of confusion must have been clear on my face because Bryan smiled and continued.

"Mac has a tendency to strut around in his underwear. We have heating and AC, but he claims to work best when he's comfortable. I swear he'd be naked all the time if I didn't put my foot down."

They were close. Maybe I'd missed something before, and they were more than friends even. I didn't have the nerve to ask, so I left it alone for another day.

"You don't have to worry about him. Mac, I mean. He's… a lot at first, but he's really sweet and open-minded."

Seeing the adoration in Bryan's eyes and the hint of a smile on his lips, I knew anyone he had to be close to would be decent. "I'd like to meet him one day. Until then, how about we watch *The Empire Strikes Back*? I'm eager to see your reaction to it."

"Ah, yes. The primary reason for me being here. Let me clean up my mess and I'll be good to go."

I insisted on Bryan not cleaning after cooking, but he didn't want to leave my kitchen a mess. We settled on both cleaning before sitting down on the couch to watch the movie. I was far more relaxed than I was for the first one and really enjoyed discreetly watching Bryan's reactions out of the corner of my eye. He offered some commentary during the movie, which I was surprised didn't annoy me. Hearing—and seeing—how much he was into it only enhanced the experience of re-watching for me. Nothing was too loud or over-the-top until near the end when Luke and Vader were fighting. Knowing what was coming, I shifted all of my attention from the TV over to Bryan. His eyes were wide with wonder, and he looked like a child experiencing something new and exciting for the first time.

He shot out a lively "oh, fuck" when Luke's hand was cut off, and I practically vibrated beside him in anticipation of what was to come. When Vader said his most famous line, Bryan's jaw literally dropped open on a sharp gasp. He remained silent for the rest of the movie then turned toward me when the credits popped up. I turned the volume down and felt the corners of my mouth curve upward.

Bryan ran his hands through his hair then along his jaw, the scrape from his beard audible. "Hoooooly shit. That was intense." He looked down at Prince, on the couch between us; she was watching him. "Did you know that was coming? I've heard that line misquoted and tossed around, but seeing the scene play out like that was… wow. You should have given me a heads-up." Turning his attention back to me, Bryan said, "That was ridiculous. That was sooooo much better than the first one. I have so many questions. Is Han going to be all right after being frozen like that? Who is that bounty hunter dude? Gah."

"Is that all?" I asked with an amused lilt to my voice.

"Ford got hotter," he muttered.

I snorted from laughing, my hand flying up to my nose as if I could pull the sound back in.

"What's that badass music that plays when Vader is around?"

"That would be 'The Imperial March.'"

"I need to download that. Shit. You said there's one more from the original movies?" He sounded so hopeful and young—not at all the threat I initially thought him to be— funny how perceptions can be altered so quickly.

"There's one more. *Return of the Jedi.*"

"When can we watch that one? I don't think I can wait another week." He'd shifted to querulous, demonstrating once again how wrong I was about him before. The new sides of Bryan were fascinating, and I found myself not yet wanting to be finished with his company.

"We can watch the next one right now, if you want to," I offered.

"Really?" The optimism in his voice made me bite back a

smile. "What about Prince? Don't you guys have to go for a run?"

"I already took her before the movie. I… I didn't want to be rude and rush you out like I did before. Sorry about that. I didn't realize what I was doing." I swallowed hard and held Bryan's gaze. I needed him to know I didn't mean anything by my prior actions.

"Don't worry about that, Eli. I could tell you didn't mean anything by it. I promise it takes more to offend me." He offered an easy smile, dimples and all, so I took his word and nodded. "And yeah, I'd love to watch the next one if you're cool with that."

Of course I was. Bryan refreshed our drinks and movie snacks while I took Prince out for a quick bathroom break then we were back on the couch. Prince took the far left cushion, sprawling out and resting her head on the arm rest, so I sat next to Bryan and hoped he wouldn't think it was weird. I was pretty tense, caught up in wondering if I should have just made Prince move or asked if he minded. By the time the movie started I realized I was too far inside my head again; Bryan wasn't remotely uncomfortable with my presence, and I needed to relax. I opened my beer, leaned back into the cushions, and paid no mind to how my shoulder touched Bryan's, or how our knees occasionally bumped.

SIX

BRYAN

"**B**RO, WHAT ARE YOU DOING?"

The alarm in Mac's voice snapped me out of my daze, and I looked down at the frying pan to see that I'd burned a pancake. "Shit, my bad." I scooped out the mess and set the pan aside to cool as Mac took a seat at the counter.

"What's on your mind? You were miles away just now."

I took a deep breath and recounted the events of my evening with Eli. I downplayed how much my pulse raced when Eli sat next to me instead of at the other end of the couch. No, I didn't at all mention how much heat his body gave off, or that I needed to force myself to take steady breaths so my pulse didn't pound loud enough for Eli to hear. I tried to change the subject and discuss the movies with him, but he didn't bite.

"I can hear what you're not saying. You forget that trying to keep shit from me is pointless." He scratched at the short blond scruff along his jaw while eyeing me knowingly.

I sighed because it was all I could do. Like he'd said, there was no point in leaving parts of the truth out or lying. "I care about him. Believe me, I'm not going to act on it—that never works out." To say I crashed and burned in my previous attempts at romancing straight men would be an egregious understatement, although the last time was the worst. That guy had a pregnant girlfriend I didn't know about and strung me along until the baby was born. I vowed not to make that mistake again, and Mac vowed never to let me make it.

"You can try some distance? You guys hanging out is new. Slow it down before it's too late and you're miserable."

I vehemently shook my head and braced my hands against the edge of the counter. "No, I can't do that. First of all, I don't want to hurt Eli in any way. He doesn't put himself out there often, and it would probably crush him to be rejected after doing so."

"Perhaps you're singing your praises a bit too highly?" Mac deadpanned.

"Shut it," I said with only mild frustration. "Second, I don't want to see him less. If anything, I want to see him more."

"But it's okay for you to get hurt?"

My gut reaction was to say that I wouldn't, but I knew it was a rhetorical question, and by getting defensive I'd be adding more weight to Mac's already valid point of view. I took a couple of deep, calming breaths and chose my next words carefully. "We can't know for sure that I will. I'm friends with plenty of straight guys I don't want to fuck, and—"

"Who said anything about fucking? Got something on the brain?" Mac asked, the triumph clearly detectable in his voice.

He was right, and I couldn't deny it, so I did what any well-adjusted, mature adult would do and flipped him off.

"I don't want you to get in over your head, Bry. I love

you like a brother, but you're borderline unbearable when you're all mopey. If it happens again, I might actually smother you in your sleep." His smile softened his words, but his warning was clear. I was pretty sure we both already knew I was past the point of heeding his warnings though.

"I hear you. I do."

"Good." Mac slid down across the counter until his face was pressed against it. "If we're done having a moment, are you going to finish making breakfast before I die?"

A much-needed laugh rolled through me, and I ruffled Mac's hair before moving the cooled pan back onto the front burner. Mac put on some music—"I Am a God" by Kanye— and booted up his laptop before coming back over to the kitchen to eat the hot raspberry pancakes I'd just served up. He thanked me and dug right in before I'd even set the syrup in front of him.

"So," he began, "when do I get to meet your new friend?"

I poured more batter into the pan and watched bubbles immediately begin to break the surface. "I'm not sure. We briefly talked about him coming over here last night and he said he'd like to." Mac's eyes went wide and he sucked in an excited gasp, but I shut that shit down. "If he comes over here do you promise to play nice?"

Mac scoffed and took another bite of his breakfast. "I'm always nice—I'm like a fucking golden retriever."

"You know what I mean."

"Yes, Dad. I'll be on my best behavior."

I piled another pancake on his plate and turned the burner off. "Hurry up and finish. I want your opinion on the space before we go to the game." We were playing against some of Axel's friends in a few hours. They were a decent team, but we were better.

"You want my opinion? Pick a name for your damn bakery, already."

I smirked and waggled my brows. "That's part of what you're going to be helping me with. Bring clothes; you can get dirty too."

ELI WARNED me to have an open mind when we watched *The Phantom Menace* a few days later. It definitely wasn't what I was expecting, and the Jar Jar guy was kind of annoying, though Darth Maul made up for it with his sheer badassery. Oh, and Liam Neeson and Ewan McGregor. Eli looked about ready to rage-quit the movie every time Jar Jar opened his mouth—it was equal parts hilarious and adorable, and I didn't even bother trying not to laugh.

I'd cooked again that night and discovered that Eli had strong feelings against onions. I persuaded him that the dish needed them then spent most of my prep time all but mincing them into a paste. My extra efforts were well worth it when we sat down to eat and Eli's face lit up after the first bite of spaghetti primavera. He'd conceded that onions weren't so bad after that.

Mac had been helping me with the bakery nearly every day for at least a couple of hours—and we'd even come up with a name. I had a meeting with Eli at noon to go over some early plans and tell him about the name I'd chosen. We could have done it by email just fine, but I wanted to see him and show him how the kitchen was coming along. With half an hour until Eli was set to arrive, I halted work and released Mac from his task of painting the walls and ceiling. He guessed that Eli was coming by and teased me for being a lovesick puppy before he finally did leave.

Eli showed up ten minutes ahead of schedule and came straight back to the kitchen at my request. I'd like to think he looked extremely happy to see me, but that was probably me reading too far into a simple smile and friendly greeting.

"Whoa, you've made a lot of progress from a couple weeks ago," Eli said, his head darting around, taking in the brand-new commercial appliances and counters. His eyes stopped on the half-painted wall Mac had been working on. "Do you need any help finishing up painting?"

The half-painted wall was white, and I had off-white paint all over my hands and clothes so it was pretty clear I hadn't been the one working on that space. "You don't have to. I'm not about to turn down the help or company, though. Mac was here earlier, but he's been helping out all week, and I sent him home." *So we could meet in private.*

"We can look at my ideas when we're finished painting. I don't have any other appointments this afternoon, so I've got nowhere to be."

I set Eli up with one of my old T-shirts, which hung loose on his lean body in a way that made my mind go straight to the gutter. I'd been trying not to let my thoughts of Eli stray, and I didn't let myself think about the video of us a few keyboard strokes away out of respect for him. But seeing him wearing my clothes did something to me I couldn't control. I wanted to pin him to the counter and rip his clothes off to get access to that expanse of smooth skin I was unable to forget.

Eli's unassuming smile snapped me out of my thoughts, and I found myself feeling guilty. Betraying his friendship wasn't an option and I had to try harder to keep my thoughts in order. It wasn't his fault that my control was slipping, but it would be a problem for both of us if I didn't smarten the hell up and rein it in.

I set him up with fresh brushes, instructions, and a ladder then went back to the walls I was working on. We chatted for the first few minutes then I put on some music, which only made me imagine that we were in a movie and we'd have a cute paint-fight montage and then have se—

No. No, no, no. Shutting that shit down.

God, I was reverting back to my teenaged self all over a damn T-shirt. That wasn't entirely true, was it? It was all Eli, and that was what Mac had tried to warn me about. Ugh, oh well. I'd already decided I wouldn't stop seeing him, so I'd deal with my new problem a different way.

As if he had telepathy and sensed my inner struggle, Mac texted me.

M: Have you jumped him yet?
B: That's not funny
M: Ouch. That bad, huh

I peeked over my shoulder at Eli and saw he was dutifully painting, like I should have been.

B: It could be worse
B: But I really don't wanna know how much worse it could get
M: We're going out tonight

Huh?

B: Way to change the subject
M: Nope. Still on topic
M: Gonna get you laid and distracted

I sighed and shook my head, even if Mac couldn't see it. It had been about two months since I'd hooked up with anyone, which was a bit for me. Between buying the space for the bakery and getting together a business plan, I'd been busy. Then I met Eli and stopped thinking about sex alto-gether—then today happened.

B: We can talk about it when I get home. Gotta get back to work

M: Love youuuuuu. Keep your mitts to yourself, you bad man, you

B: LY2

I cringed and pocketed my phone, going back to the task at hand as if it were the most captivating thing I'd ever done.

To escape the smell of drying paint, Eli and I went back to the bar we'd patronized a few weeks ago. Eli showed me his research on market trends and explained what was in and what was anticipated to be popular. It was well outside of my scope, but I trusted Eli and it all sounded lovely. He spoke with a confidence I only ever heard when he was in "work mode" or answering my many *Star Wars* questions.

Eli finished explaining as our server dropped off two burger platters and a couple of bottles of beer. I dove into my fries, clearly having underestimated my need for food throughout the day, only stopping when Eli's faint laughter reached my ears.

"What? I'm starving."

"I'm not judging you. I'm just a little surprised, that's all."

"About what?" I asked before introducing more tasty fries to my mouth.

"Ah, well, you're pretty fit, but you eat a lot of food that doesn't seem conducive with that lifestyle. Your cooking is healthy, but then you eat two plates of it, and you got extra fries today and—I'm sorry. I'm being rude as hell."

I'd been holding it in, but I cracked and burst into laugh-ter, nearly choking in the process. The tips of Eli's ears reddened while he downed half of his beer. "You're not rude. You're pretty blunt and direct, though I respect that. You say exactly what's on your mind when you're not thinking too much, even if it is a little funny sometimes. I looooove food. It's probably my number one vice, far above anything else... well, except maybe sex, but even that's cutting it close. I work out a lot and cook healthy meals to combat my weakness for junk and snacks." More fries. More salty, golden, fried good-ness to distract myself from the fact that I just brought up sex, and was starting to sweat.

"I've only been inside of a gym once. I had no idea what I was doing and was convinced people were talking about me. I lasted about fifteen minutes before I had to leave, and I haven't set foot in one since. It sounds so stupid when I say it out loud." Eli rolled his eyes and took a bite from his burger. "I don't know why I haven't gone back. That incident was about eight years ago."

"What do you want from it?"

"Is that a serious question? Look at you. You look amaz-ing. I don't think I could ever get to be your size, but a bit of bulk would probably do wonders for my self-esteem."

There he went again with his unfiltered way of speaking. And did he really think I looked amazing? Best not to dwell on that comment. "If you want some pointers or a workout buddy, I'm sure we can figure out a time. That said, don't think you're lesser for not going. With all the running you do I bet you have way better endurance than me and plenty of lean muscle. Trust me when I say that you don't need to be bigger to feel good about yourself." Or to be desirable.

"You're probably right. Anyway, you said there was some-thing you wanted to tell me?"

I'd forgotten all about that. I explained how Mac had been giving me a hand and that we'd come up with a name a few days ago.

"Eat Cake," I said, motioning with my hands for emphasis. It appealed to the pervert in me while also being direct, not making people guess what we sold.

Eli's brow furrowed, and he chewed on his thumbnail. His deep-in-thought face was pretty cute, even if it did make me nervous. "I like it," he finally said. "It's catchy, snappy, bold. Have you given any thought to the appearance of the logo?"

Did he not catch the obvious sexual innuendo with the name? *Interesting.* "Not yet. I wanted your opinion before I committed to hiring someone."

"Would you mind if I took a stab at it? You don't have to use anything I design, but I have an idea I'd like to flesh out."

Of course I said yes. I didn't know that Eli had graphic design skills. I'd assumed his job would be to generate ideas then pass them off to a different department to be drawn or rendered, or whatever. I'd jump at the chance to see something artist Eli created—especially something just for me.

Seemingly pleased with my answer, Eli went back to work on his burger and asked me more questions about the bakery and color schemes. I was sad to see him go when we finished up, but I didn't let it show when we parted.

MAC WASN'T KIDDING when he'd said we were going out. By the time I got home Axel was sitting on the couch with our friend Blake—no doubt trying to flirt with her—and Maxim was going to meet us at the club. Mac had assembled the singles' crew, and there would be no getting out of going tonight. I didn't bother trying to fight Mac on why I didn't need to go and instead showered and changed into a pair of dark-wash fitted jeans and a green-and-black tank. I'd assumed we were going to go to a gay club, since the idea was to get me laid. For being straight, Mac had no qualms about exclusively going to gay bars when we went out. He'd always managed to find women and lay on his charm. Blake and Maxim would have no problem with going to a gay club, but I wondered if Mac told Axel what he was signing up for. Knowing my best friend, he probably withheld that detail for his own amusement.

Satisfied with my appearance, I moved back out to the living room and sat down next to Axel. His wavy black hair had recently been cut into a clean taper fade, making him even cuter than when he had his hair shagged out. He didn't look quite as young with his hair shorter, but he still looked pretty damn young. He'd attributed his baby face to him being Mexican, and said that his dad also looked younger than he was, which was wild to me. Puberty had hit me harder than a freight train; I went from fifteen to thirty over a few months and have looked more or less the same ever since. I gained more muscle mass over the years, but that was about the only change.

It was way too early to go out, so we piled into Mac's bed and took turns playing two-player racing and fighting games until it was time to leave. Maxim, true to his word, was waiting outside when we arrived. A little taller than me with brown eyes and dark brown hair, Maxim was hot. We never clicked sexually, and were much better as friends.

Blake and Mac walked up last with Mac's arm around her shoulders and her arm around his waist. They used to have a thing, but they were just friends now—*sans* benefits. Seeing them together was too much pretty blond in one place and was rather sickening anyway.

Mac pulled his arm from Blake's shoulders and led us inside, paying the cover for our whole group. The pounding music could be felt before it was heard as we entered the building and made our way downstairs to the dance floor.

Stale air smelling of smoke and sweat thickened the closer we got to the music until we stepped into the throng of dancing bodies. Mac and Maxim went to go get some drinks while Axel looked at the crowd of mostly men—in various states of undress—with wide eyes.

He stepped close to me and stood on his toes to speak into my ear. "Mac promised he'd be my wingman tonight—how the fuck am I supposed to get laid when there are no girls here?"

I felt a little, just a little, bad for him. I sought out Blake, and she winked at me after waggling her manicured eyebrows at Axel. Yeah, he'd be all right—that didn't mean I wouldn't fuck with him a bit.

"I don't know, Axe, your new haircut is pretty damn cute. I could probably find you twenty guys who'd be interested." I was teasing, but that didn't make it any less true.

"Bry," he whined.

"Relax. Mac won't try to set you up with any guys. Stick with us and you likely won't get hit on too much."

"I can live with a guy coming on to me," he muttered.

Someone approaching from behind Axel caught my eye and the way he'd checked out Axel's ass was impossible to miss. "I hope you mean that because an interested party is on the way over," I warned.

Blake and I stepped back and observed with a smile while Axel grinned and all but blushed, too distracted to see that someone else had approached.

"Hey," he said to me.

He was cute—about five foot nine with dirty blond hair, freckles, and big brown eyes. His eyes locked with mine, and I could see the heat in them.

"Hey," I returned.

He made the usual small talk and asked for my name, which I gave him. His was Charlie, and he was a twenty-two-year-old nursing student. After a couple of minutes of the age-old song and dance, he suggested we leave and go have some fun. I'd politely declined, saying I was just out to dance with friends. He was disappointed, though he moved on and was swallowed into the crowd. Any other time, I'd have been all over a guy like him. Any other time, I wouldn't have cared about the color of his eyes. Now it was all I could see. A pair of pretty brown eyes, but not the ones I wanted most.

SEVEN

ELI

AFTER SKETCHING AN INITIAL CONCEPT for Bryan's logo, I decided to do a traditional mock-up instead of going straight to a 3D rendering. My preferred medium was always ink and watercolors, but I hadn't used either in years and needed to buy more—which was how I found myself at an art supply store after work. I purchased black ink, an array of paint colors, and thick card stock. The canvases felt too daunting. I still had a large, blank one tucked away in my closet under a sheet as if it were a portrait displaying all of my grotesque sins.

With the required supplies in hand and a good chunk of money missing from my account, I left the store and headed home. Like always, I changed clothes and took Prince out for a long run. I wasn't in the mood to cook, so I picked up some take-out chicken tacos on the way home, which I devoured before I even showered. I got one with diced onions to try, but they were too crunchy and overpowering. I'd stick with skipping onions unless Bryan was the one doing the cooking.

Bryan. He kept me on my toes like no one else ever had. Best of all, he put up with my stupid mouth and didn't easily take offense. Offending people and being rude was never my intent, but when I reflected on the things I sometimes said, it was clear how the recipients could have taken them as negative. Eve called me out on it as it happened so I could get better at recognizing when I was saying tone-deaf things. I thought it had been working until I met Bryan. It seemed that my capacity to say the wrong things to him was endless, yet he always just smiled or laughed it off like it was the most amusing thing. *And* he liked Prince. There wasn't anything more I could ask for in a friend.

Volunteering to do the logo for Eat Cake was a way for me to give back for all Bryan's friendship had given me. It bothered me to think that only I was benefitting from us being friends but figuring out what I could possibly offer him in return left me without answers—until talks of the logo started. If he decided not to use it, I at least hoped it would give him some direction with what he wanted. I'd be lying if I said I didn't care if he liked it, though. I really wanted to create something he'd enjoy.

I hadn't thought about painting in years. It was something I used to do for my mom before she died. After I lost her it became something I associated with pain—and not that useful tortured-artist type of pain where the best work of a person's career was created. I was crippled by the thought of looking at a canvas, much less holding a brush.

When I got hired at Red Right Hand, I did some work with ink but stuck to 3D renderings and sketches for all other art and promotional materials. After Eve's engagement party last year, I stopped into an art store and drunkenly bought a huge canvas, thinking that was a good idea. When I got it home, I'd sobered up enough to know that it had been a mistake. And that was how it ended up in my bedroom closet under a sheet.

I knew I wasn't ready to uncover it, but the fact that I wanted to paint again thrilled and nauseated me in equal parts. With Prince at my feet, I opened the new ink and paints and swallowed down my trepidation as I made the first brushstroke against the cardstock.

"I painted last night," I said to Eve.

Her mouth opened into an O and her eyes went wide. "That's great, pet. What brought that on?" She tasted a plate of chicken masala, one of five dishes on the table in front of us. We were at the caterer choosing her wedding menu on a Thursday afternoon. It wasn't too often that I got hauled out to these events, but Samir had to work and I'd never be selfish enough to make Eve go on her own. Also, the food was free and much more enticing than the tuna wrap I had packed.

"I made a logo design for Bryan's bakery. I don't know if he'll like it, but I think it looks good."

She halted the forkful of risotto inches from her mouth and turned in her chair to face me. "Why didn't you tell me this morning?"

I looked around the room to make sure there was no one else in earshot. We were in a private room for the tasting and we were alone, but it was a habit. "I didn't want someone to overhear."

She sighed knowingly and bumped my arm with her elbow. "Were you hired to do the logo?"

"No. I kind of asked to do it. As a favor." I picked up my fork and stabbed a pillowy piece of ravioli and muttered, "I thought it would be a nice thing to do for him." I popped the pasta in my mouth and was surprised with the flavors of spinach and ricotta. There were three different fillings on the plate and I hadn't been paying enough attention to remember what the options were. As I swallowed that first bite, I found myself wondering if Bryan knew how to make ravioli. I bet he did. I'd been beginning to wonder if there was anything he couldn't do—not in a hyperbolic sense, although that really wouldn't surprise me.

Eve rested her chin on my shoulder and blinked her blue eyes up at me. "I'm proud of you, Elijah."

"What? Why?"

"For stepping outside your bubble and taking a chance on someone new. You know I worry about you being alone so much." She brushed my hair behind my ear like no one had since I lost my mom. It was soothing in a way I hadn't realized I missed. "You really fancy Bryan. You've taken to him pretty quick."

I shrugged noncommittally, but it was true.

"Oh, come on. It took me almost two months before you'd give me more than your resting-bitch face when I'd try to strike up conversation."

I wrinkled my nose and scoffed. "I do *not* have resting-bitch face."

"No, you don't. I'm fairly certain you were giving me active-bitch face so I'd leave you alone. Lucky for you it didn't work." Eve kissed my cheek then pulled back, turning her attention to a plate of couscous, asparagus, and salmon. "Don't think I didn't notice that you didn't answer me. I think it's wonderful that you've made a new friend."

Hearing her say it like that made me feel like the biggest loser. I didn't regret the choices I'd made that kept me distanced from people. Most people in my experience weren't like Eve and Bryan. Even so, it was a reminder that I wasn't "normal" in the sense that I wasn't conforming to societal standards of what a twenty-eight-year-old man should be. It might have been commendable if it was intentional on my part. I wanted to feel normal, and Bryan was a big help with that.

"I just don't want to screw it up," I sighed.

"You won't. Just be yourself. And try this fuckin' salmon. Sam would never agree to this, but that doesn't mean we can't keep pretending."

Eve held up her fork for me with a piece of the flaky fish. I bit it off and slowly chewed at first, unsure of what to expect. I wasn't a huge fan of fish, but that bite was pretty decent.

"Do I get to see the logo you painted?"

"Can I show you on Monday? Bryan is coming over tomorrow night and I'm going to show him then."

Eve swallowed a forkful of couscous and nodded her head, stray red strands framing her soft features. "Of course, pet. Should we order more samples? The jerk chicken sounds interesting."

We took an extended lunch and spent the rest of the afternoon stuffing ourselves and getting sloshed on pink sparkling wine, which Eve insisted tasted better.

Bryan came over a little later than what I'd established to be the usual. He apologized and said Mac had a crisis and he couldn't leave earlier—something about an angry ex and stilettos flying through bedroom windows. Again, reinforcement that being single wasn't so bad.

We didn't make dinner plans, so I'd cooked while I waited for him. The folder with the logo burned a hole through my lap while I'd been holding it and was tossed onto the counter. Bryan's eyes sought it out before quickly flicking back to me to answer my question about dinner.

"If you keep feeding me like this, you're never going to get rid of me," he said with a lopsided grin, just one dimple pooling in his left cheek.

I wasn't sure how to respond to that. Saying that I didn't want to be rid of him might have come off as creepy, and if I joked about *not* wanting him around it might have fallen flat and that would have been awful. I settled on what I hoped was a casual laugh and turned to plate up some food for us. It wasn't smooth or subtle at all, and I could feel Bryan's eyes boring holes into my back.

I should say something.

But what? Had it been too long to reply? It would probably have made the situation more awkward than I'd already made it. Maybe silence was best until—

"You're thinkin' too much," Bryan drawled in a Texas accent his normal speech lacked.

I spun around on the balls of my feet and mouthed the beginnings of "how," but my voice refused to cooperate with me. I cleared my throat and tried again. "How did you know that?"

"The set of your shoulders mostly. Your movements as well. Your shoulders carry a lot of tension when you're nervous or thinking. What's on your mind?" Bryan asked, sounding sincerely interested as he watched me from his seat across the island.

I pushed the plate and a fork in front of Bryan and leaned forward with my palms gripping the edge of the counter. "I was thinking about what you said about me not being able to get rid of you."

Surprise flashed across his face, and it was gone just as quickly. "Oh."

"Yeah, so, I know it was a joke, but I wasn't sure what to say."

"Because…"

"Because I guess I don't want to be rid of you. It sounded… weird to say that in my head. And now you're looking at me like I've got two heads, and I *know* I shouldn't have said it." I turned back around and plated my own food, needing a break from the conversation before I made it worse or passed out from embarrassment.

"I don't think that's weird. You surprised me, but it's not weird. In fact, I'd say we're very much on the same page." His voice was steady, and he spoke with a certainty I doubted I'd ever feel.

I chanced a look over my shoulder, feeling immediate relief when I took in Bryan's mouth curved into a smile. "Yeah?"

"Yeah."

I nodded to him and resumed fixing my plate before getting us each a beer and taking a seat next to him. We ate in a comfortable silence for a few minutes while I replayed our exchange to analyze where I went wrong and how I could avoid it in the future, but I kept getting stuck on that sudden burst of Texasness.

"So, what was up with that accent? Your file says you're from Texas, but you don't normally have an accent."

Bryan swallowed down a bite of the rice pilaf I'd made and grinned. "My daddy used to say that to me when I was a boy. The first time was when he was teaching me to ride horses and there was this really feisty one named Buck that I was scared of. My brothers had all ridden him when they were my age, and it was a kind of rite of passage. Was scared as hell, but my daddy's words were enough to get me to relax and act."

Daddy—must have been a Texas thing. It was kind of endearing. "What happened? Did you ride the horse?"

Bryan nodded and smiled wide enough for the corners of his eyes to crinkle. "I did. And true to his name, he bucked me off. It took me seven attempts before I was able to get him under control. Anyway, I wasn't sure if it would have the same effect without the accent."

I snorted a laugh and hummed. "I'd say it helped. I was pretty deep in my head."

"I hope you'll always say what's on your mind."

The idea of doing that was foreign to me, but I was willing to try—and that was what I told him. We finished eating and moved over to the couch to be more comfortable. I had the folder with the logo in my hand and clung to it for dear life.

"Is that what I think it is?" Bryan asked with a lip-biting smile.

"Yes. It's, uh, painted. If you like it, I can do it on the computer and make it better." I still held onto the folder, not quite ready to let it go.

"You paint? Other than walls I mean."

A laugh escaped me, which helped to ease the tension in my shoulders that I was now acutely aware of. "I do—I did. I used to paint a lot when I was in high school and university. It's been a long time, though." I took a deep breath and handed—shoved—the folder to Bryan before I chickened out and tossed it out the window.

I could see that he wanted to ask about my painting, and perhaps why I stopped, but I was glad that he didn't. I hoped I didn't give him a death glare to ward him off the topic. Knowing me, I probably did.

He licked his lips and spared me one more reassuring grin before he flipped the manila folder open. I turned my head away at the last minute, unprepared to see a potential look of disappointment on his face. As such, I couldn't see his expression, but I sure heard him gasp. He was too quiet for too long, and my curiosity got the best of me. I tilted my head in his direction to sneak a peek, my eyes widening in response to what I saw; Bryan's lips were parted, and his brow was ever so slightly furrowed and raised in shock? Surprise? I wasn't sure which, but it definitely wasn't the dissatisfaction that I was dreading.

"You painted this?" he finally asked, forehead creasing more as he turned his head toward me.

I nodded and rubbed my clammy hands across the tops of my thighs. "D-do you like it? I can make some changes if you—"

"Stop. It's perfect. This is… beautiful." He turned his attention back to the logo, smiled, then looked me in the eye. "Thank you."

I knew I should have said "you're welcome" to be polite, but I was stunned by disbelief and ground my teeth instead. "Do you really like it?" I asked, unable to hide how shaky my voice was.

"I do. It's everything I could have wanted. The blend of colors is amazing. It's eye-catching, and maybe I'm reading into it, but you've included all of the colors of the rainbow, which reminds me of Pride, though not in an overt or obnoxious kind of way. The colors are there, but it's subtle."

I had indeed included all the colors of the rainbow. The words "Eat Cake" were outlined in thick black ink and filled with a confetti pattern of watercolor paints of various dilutions. "I diluted some of the colors so they wouldn't be quite as strong. But yes, I was thinking of the rainbow motif. You've got neutral colors for the interior, save for some accents and the flowers you mentioned. Having a bold logo is a smart move. It also… reminded me of you."

Bryan cocked an eyebrow at me, and I flushed, realizing

what I'd implied. "Not because you're gay. I swear I wasn't thinking of that. You're just… you. Unapologetic and just so effortlessly who you are. Confident yet laid-back and always… just you." My words quieted near the end.

"That's how you see me?" he asked.

I nodded again. "It is."

"Fuck," he muttered, seemingly to himself. "I can see it with this logo. It stands out but not in an over-the-top tacky or flashy kind of way. What kind of paint is this?"

"Watercolor. It's outlined in black ink."

"Thank you. This is perfect." He smiled at me, one of those ones that deepened his dimples and showed his laugh lines.

"You're welcome. I'm so glad you like it. I can probably have a 3D render finished in a couple of days for you."

"Can't this be scanned? I really like that it's painted."

"I can do that, yes. I just figured I could make it better and perfectly symmetrical digitally. And I can manipulate how the colors blend."

Bryan shook his head, never taking his eyes from the folder. "No. This"—he motioned to the logo—"is perfect as is. How much do I owe you for the rights?"

"Oh. No, no. I made this for you. So I guess it's like a gift. Just, please don't tell Andrea—she'd have my head for giving away free services."

"I don't want you to work for free, Eli. And your boss should know what a great job you're doing."

I was flattered, but insisted on it being a gift, which resulted in us arguing back and forth until we both laughed at how absurd the situation was. We hadn't reached an agreement on whether to compensate me, though we did agree to shelve it for another day. I was surprised at myself for standing up to him, but I was glad I did. I hadn't realized what I was doing until after the fact, and I think Bryan knew too by the way he grinned at me. If he knew, he had the decency not to embarrass me by bringing it up and just let me feel surprised and proud of myself.

We ended up talking on the couch for about an hour longer about nothing in particular before Bryan went home, leaving me and Prince alone in an overly quiet apartment, which had never felt so quiet before.

EIGHT

BRYAN

T HE NEXT FEW WEEKS WERE SOME of the busiest of
my life. I was impatient and had next to no chill, so I
wanted to nail down an opening date as soon as possible. Eli
had advised not rushing it, and proposed a soft launch for
friends and some local bloggers to create buzz. Of course, his
idea was better than mine, so that was what I went with. Eli
made some flyers for local magazines and sites and contacted
several bloggers or vloggers or whatever—people who he said
would be instrumental in whether Eat Cake was a success or
a flop.

I hadn't been so nervous since my first university ball
game, which for me meant stress baking—a lot of stress
baking. Mac had loved it for the first couple of days. After
weeks of sweets being around the apartment, one day he'd
cursed me for making him fat as he swiped a cookie on his
way out the door to go to the gym for the second time
that day.

Eli had also benefited from my stress reliever. I brought
over endless containers of sweets for our next two movie
nights. We watched *Attack of the Clones* and *Revenge of the*

Sith. I didn't love the prequel trilogy as much as the original one, though they improved with each movie and I still really enjoyed seeing more of the story. Hayden Christensen was whiny, but he was pretty damn cute, so I let it slide more than Eli did. Stealing glances at him whenever he got frustrated was a favorite of mine.

He continued to sit next to me on the couch, even when Prince wasn't adorably hogging the space at the far end. Being that close to him was exhilarating. I noticed that he had more flat moles on his jaw, just tiny little speckles that I wanted to kiss and nip at until he—nope. I promised myself I wouldn't go there and I was trying really fucking hard not to break that. Aside from the stray thought here and there and some, uh, involuntary physiological responses, I'd been doing okay.

My will had been seriously tested a week ago while we were watching *Revenge of the Sith*. Prince had climbed in my lap for the first time while I was on the couch, waiting for Eli to come in with some spinach dip he made. By the time Eli came in, Prince had made my lap into her personal doggie bed and was curled up in a tight little ball. Eli all but melted when he saw us and even took a picture to show Eve, whom I'd come to know as his colleague and best friend. I hadn't been back to Red Right Hand since our initial meeting, so I hadn't had the pleasure of meeting her. She sounded like a good person from how Eli spoke of her. Knowing he had someone else who cared for him helped put my mind at ease when I wasn't around. It wasn't that I thought he needed me —I   wasn't   *that*   self-involved—but   everybody needed *someone* at least some of the time. I hoped I would be able to be that for Eli, and I was glad that he already had someone. He never talked about his parents or any siblings, which I took as a cue to leave the subject alone.

Twenty minutes into the movie, Eli had reached over my

lap to pet Prince and my blood turned to ice as panic set in. With his hand moving that close to my dick, I was unable to control my bodily reaction. I'd shifted Prince onto Eli's lap and quickly excused myself to the washroom to calm down. I'd done my fair share of questionable things in my life, but jerking off in a friend's bathroom because I was sexually frustrated was a box I'd yet to check—and one I'd rather not. After a lot of cold water and reciting recipes in my head, my dick decided to cooperate with me and I was able to rejoin Eli and Prince. Eli had paused the movie and was on his phone when I returned, looking all too unnatural in his posture to have been casually checking the device. Knowing him, he'd picked it up when he heard the toilet flush to be polite and pretend he'd been distracted while I was gone. I didn't want him feeling awkward about his actions, so I addressed the situation with a lie, because there was no way I could say "sorry I popped a boner like a horny teenager and had to bolt." In that instance, feigning sickness seemed to be the lesser of two evils, so that's what I went with. After assuring Eli that I was okay, we resumed the movie and Prince crawled back in my lap with a sleepy huff. It was due to sheer force of will that I didn't have to dart away for the rest of the movie while Eli was petting his dog.

When I got home that night I went straight for my room and jerked off twice while biting my pillow to keep quiet. Mac not so discreetly told me to put music on next time or he was going to record audio of me "pleasuring myself" and save it for a prime opportunity. Knowing him, that meant the next time our friends were over and he was drunk. I'd have been horrified if it had been anyone else, but Mac had walked in on me doing much worse over the years, so this was nothing. I baked him a dozen macarons as an apology and giggled while he mumbled compliments peppered with expletives as he ate them all.

A FEW DAYS after my peace-offering macarons, I found myself in the finished kitchen of Eat Cake baking even more —along with cakes, pies, cookies, and brownies—to test the functionality of my new equipment. I'd just pulled out a sheet of coconut chocolate chip cookies when my phone rang from across the kitchen. I made quick work of sliding the cookies onto a cooling rack and answered the call before it reached voicemail, offering a breathy generic greeting.

"Evenin', little brother. Didya forget me already?" my eldest brother's voice greeted, thick with the accent I'd shed years ago.

"Hey. What's up, O?"

Owen sighed into the phone and told me about the new calves that were born a few weeks ago. Calving season meant he'd been even busier than usual, tending to the mothers and new additions to the herd. There were always some who were born underweight or got sick and needed extra care. He updated me on Mason and Chase, my other brothers, and all the goings on around town I'd have been privy to had I not moved away. I loved my family dearly and I enjoyed working on the ranch, but it wasn't the life I wanted for myself, and I always knew that. My parents weren't happy when I told them I was moving away for university, but they supported me and respected my decision all the same.

"How's your bakery coming along? Mama said you had some guys in doing some work a couple weeks ago? Ya coulda called us to come help."

"I appreciate that, and I know you guys would have come, but y'all have your hands full enough out there." My brothers had always been supportive of me, even after I came out. Hell, especially after I came out.

"S'ppose you're right," Owen drawled. I could practically see him shrugging as he often did when he conceded.

"Why don't y'all come visit me once the calves are a bit older and things calm down?"

"Ah'ite. I'll get to talk'n'ta the boys and find a time. You and Mac been gettin' on all good?"

I rolled my eyes and groaned internally. My brothers were supportive to a fault, but they didn't believe me when I told them Mac was *just* my best friend. I doubted they'd even heard me any time I mentioned he was straight. Mac didn't help matters by not discouraging my brothers' theories any time they'd met. "Mac is his usual self, so we're fine. He made me a website for the bakery in exchange for a chocolate cheesecake. And I, uh, met someone new."

"You don't say? Got yourself a fella finally?" Owen's voice took on a brighter tone.

"No, it's not like that. We're just friends."

"But I reckon you're fixin' to change that."

I sighed. There was no point in trying to lie to Owen—he always knew. "I really like him, O. He's not gay, though. I think I'm destined for unrequited love," I muttered.

"Love, huh? You that sweet on him?" Owen asked.

Shit. Was I? I'd been trying not to think about it, but that didn't change my feelings whatsoever. "Yeah, I think I'm fallin' for him."

Owen was quiet for a few moments, likely shocked at the sincerity in my voice. Aside from a high school boyfriend, he hadn't heard me say I loved anyone before. I had plenty of healthy relationships, but love had never been a factor. Fear of commitment was not an issue for me, I just didn't click in a way I saw as long lasting with any of my former partners. With Eli I felt a spark. I knew things could be different with him. I knew from the first moment I spoke to him ten years ago.

"Tell me about him. I got lots'a time t'night."

Eli texted me a couple of nights later while I was playing *Call of Duty* with Mac in his room. I'd been losing miserably and was glad for the excuse to take a break. I went to my room and collapsed on the bed with a fresh beer in hand and opened my messages.

E: Hi… Just a couple quick things. I secured you an interview with someone at *Chicago* magazine next Tuesday. I'll tell you more about it when I see you

E: And I was checking to see if you were still coming over to watch *Rogue One* on Friday? No problem if you're busy

Hoooooooly shit! Chicago was the biggest lifestyle magazine in the city. This interview was a huge fucking deal and not at all something I was expecting. My thumbs flew across the touchscreen fast enough that the auto-correct worked overtime.

B: ARE YOU SERIOUS?! You're the fucking best!

E: I am being serious. I wouldn't lie to you or joke about this

Ugh, he was so adorable.

B: That's amazing. You're amazing. Thank you so much

E: You don't have to thank me. It's my job

B: You're too humble

B: Don't even try to deny it

E: …okay

B: I'm totally still coming over on Friday btw. Do you mind if I come by a bit earlier?

E: Sure. I'll be home by five thirty

B: See you then

I arrived at Eli's apartment building at quarter after five and waited down in the lobby. He breezed in about ten minutes later and stopped dead in his tracks when he laid eyes on me.

"Hey," I greeted.

"Hi. You're, uh, wearing shorts," he said as a flush crept up his neck from under his shirt collar.

I was indeed wearing shorts. And an orange-and-red tank top with low-cut sides. "I am. Are they too short?" They hit about mid-thigh, which was too short for my tastes for casual wear, but for running or swimming trunks it was the perfect length.

"No, no. It's not that. I'm just wondering why? I mean, you're allowed to wear shorts. You just look… sporty."

His face twisted as he cringed at his words, eliciting a laugh from me. I closed the short distance between us and slung my arm over his shoulders before I even realized what I was doing. He went stiff for a moment then relaxed, and turned to me questioningly. "Relax, Eli. I look sporty because I was hoping I could join you and Prince on your run."

"Oh. Yes, of course. She'll love that." He grinned at me, and I got lost in the sea of those rich brown eyes.

My gaze traveled down to his jaw and the few days' worth of stubble just starting to obscure those smooth, little moles that I wanted to kiss so desperately. He swallowed, and my eyes tracked the movements in his throat, all the way down to the hollow. He had more moles peeking out from under the collar of his shirt and—*Lord help me*—I wanted to know every mark on his body.

"We should go upstairs and grab her," Eli said, breaking me from my daze.

"Oh. Yeah." I dropped my arm from his shoulders, hoping he didn't notice how I'd subconsciously tightened my hold on him while I was… distracted. It would have been great if my face didn't give me away either.

"You can leave your bag inside. Come on."

We went up to Eli's apartment, dropped off our stuff, and I hooked up Prince on her leash while he changed into a T-shirt and basketball shorts. Once we got outside, he took Prince over to some grass for a quick pee while he stretched. Five minutes later we walked over to the Lakefront Trail and set off on a light jog.

"You don't have to go easy on me, you know."

Eli turned to me and smirked. "You sure you can keep up?"

"Probably not, if I'm being honest. But Prince is used to the exertion, so let's find out." I knew good and well that I couldn't keep up. We went faster and harder, but while I was a disgusting sweaty mess, he looked like he'd just run up a single flight of stairs and was mildly winded. I knew he had to have some killer endurance and stamina, though I didn't quite expect to get smoked so badly. Eli must have known how the run would go and held back. Both he and Prince were just dandy when we got back almost an hour later. I was considering whether it was plausible that I developed asthma over the past hour.

When we got up to Eli's apartment, I died. I succumbed to the jelly feeling in my legs and all but fell to the floor, and was assaulted by Prince licking my face relentlessly. My mock-protests only made it easier for her to lick my mouth. I was too damn tired to move away and didn't really care anyway, so she continued until Eli stopped laughing enough to call her away.

"Are you all right?" he asked, staring down at me with an easy smile.

I held up my right hand and gave an "OK" sign before letting my hand drop gracelessly to the floor. "I'm good," I panted shamelessly.

"Come on." Eli held his hand out to me. "Let's get you up and in the shower. I'm assuming you have a change of clothes in your bag?"

I nodded because it was all I could muster and reached up for his hand. My fingers twitched as his ran gently over my palm and wrist. The contact ignited my sense of touch, making my skin feel hot and hypersensitive everywhere his fingers grazed. I wondered if he could feel it because I could have sworn that my skin was on fire. Eli eyes scanned me up and down before he grasped my wrist and helped haul me to my feet. If I didn't know any better, I'd have said that he checked me out, but I knew that was wishful thinking.

"Thanks," I scraped out, still feeling fuzzy from his simple touch. I locked eyes with Eli and nearly got sucked into a daze again, but he turned away.

"No problem. I'll, uh, order some Chinese food to have with the movie. You like the Mongolian beef, yeah?" Eli had gotten so much better at maintaining eye contact when he spoke to me over the last couple of months. Seeing him so clearly frazzled after he hadn't said something awkward was strange. I raised an eyebrow in question. His gaze remained anywhere but on me. Whatever it was, he clearly didn't want to talk about it, so I left it alone, grabbed my bag, and headed for the shower—which I took cold.

NINE

ELI

I'D JUST FINISHED AN HOUR-LONG meeting with Andrea, going over every detail of Bryan's file and campaign. She'd told me she trusted me to make the best impression possible and thankfully didn't leave me with any parting orders. I left out that we'd become friends and stuck exclusively to our working relationship, which seemed to satisfy her.

Talking about Bryan in a professional, almost clinical manner felt wrong to me. Bryan was so much more than just my client. I didn't know exactly how to define what he was for me, but I knew the label of "client" was insufficient.

Everything surrounding Bryan was a bit of an enigma to me. He wasn't at all how I thought he should be, in all the best possible ways. Instead of being a threat, he was kind— patient and attentive and never dismissive or judgmental. He was very much like he was the first time I met him.

I was ready to pass out or vomit before he came over and introduced himself with a smile and flash of his dimples. He'd asked me if it was my first time, and I had burned hot with embarrassment at being identified as a virgin so easily.

He nudged my shoulder and told me not to worry about it, that his first time was nerve-racking too, and that it got easier. He distracted me by talking about a movie he'd recently watched with Paul Walker and some sled dogs that had made him cry. I told him I had a new puppy I rescued, and that she was sick which was why I was there that day. Bryan's eyes had lit up at the mention of a puppy, and he'd asked to see her after the shoot. I said yes after talking a bit more, and I agreed to grab a burger after the shoot too.

Then we filmed the scene, and I—

Why am I thinking about that *night?*

I hadn't thought about the details of that night in years and had the memory buried so deep in my subconscious that I'd nearly convinced myself it was a dream. Or so I thought. I started dredging up scenes from that night after I saw Bryan last week when he met me for a run. I could tell before that he was extremely fit, but that outfit... those fitted shorts and that muscle shirt left very little to the imagination. I found myself taking in his appearance and thinking he looked good —really good. I wanted to tell him, then I chickened out and instead said something stupid. That was typical for me, and Bryan didn't even blink twice, thankfully.

I caught myself taking in his appearance again while I helped him up off my floor. He looked... different somehow. New, perhaps. Bryan was attractive in a way I hadn't really noticed before. I'd gotten caught up in just observing him, though I wasn't sure why I'd done it in the first place.

That day we went running mixed with my straying thoughts to when we had se—

No. I still couldn't bring myself to think about the actual act. I did what I had to do to get Prince healthy and that was where that story was supposed to end. But Bryan, he... complicated things. Understanding why that might be so was as much a mystery as the man in question. I'd try not to stress over it. I liked what we were, and it was only natural that I wouldn't fully understand it; I'd never had a guy friend like him before, so I didn't know what to expect. Asking him crossed my mind, but I decided against it.

My reverie was disrupted by my email notification sounding off on my computer and phone. Paige Turner of *Chicago* magazine emailed me to confirm the date and time of Bryan's pre-launch in a week's time. I typed out a quick reply then sent Eve a text, thanking her once more for connecting me with Paige. I spent the rest of the day working on other files and ended up staying at the office for an extra half hour to finish some research I was doing for a hair salon opening in Lakeview in a couple of months.

By time I got home, I felt more worn out than I normally did, but I took Prince out anyway and made a mental note to pick her up some new toys. During my run, my thoughts drifted back to Bryan, which only served to confuse me further. In turn, I felt guilty for not giving Prince my undivided attention after being at work all day. She really didn't seem to mind and enjoyed our run all the same, but I felt like being distracted wasn't fair. I made an effort to pay more attention to her after we got home, but I was powerless to control my dreams that night.

IT WAS the day of the pre-launch for Eat Cake, and my anxiety was on high. I'd texted Bryan that morning to wish him good luck, and ease his nerves. The exchange had quickly morphed into him calming me down. He ended up calling me to ensure that I was okay and asked if I'd be coming by to check things out.

I'd immediately said yes, because why wouldn't I want to support my friend? He'd worked so hard to get that space ready and realize his vision, and there was no way I'd miss out on supporting him. The pre-launch was scheduled from noon till two in the afternoon, and I promised I'd be there before wishing him well and hanging up.

Making promises over the phone was fine and dandy. Rounding the corner to the bakery reminded me that there would be a room full of strange people that I sincerely did not want to face. I'd been by last week, but the sign hadn't been up yet. Seeing it while my stomach was already in knots over the social outing had a strange effect on me; I felt a weird mix of pride and embarrassment at seeing my painted logo emblazoned on the bakery's sign for the world to see. I'd never put my personal art "out there" before and, although no one would know—or care—that the logo was mine, it still made me nauseous. Despite that, I was insanely proud of Bryan and happy to have been able to create something he loved. I was proud of that, even if I couldn't shake my negative reaction.

Someone bumped my shoulder, generating an automatic apology from me and making me realize that I couldn't continue to stand on the fucking sidewalk like a light pole. I took a few deep breaths on my way up to the door, pulled it open, and stepped inside.

The weight of the room immediately hit me, making me jittery and wanting to turn and walk out. There were more people present than I'd expected, which shouldn't have surprised me too much. Bryan had to have a lot of friends, and of course they'd want to be there to support him, just as I was. Even so, I considered leaving and texting Bryan the biggest apology when my eyes found him. He was talking to a short brunette woman I recognized as being Paige Turner. He smiled at something she said, and in that moment I knew I wasn't going anywhere. As much as I wanted to run, I wouldn't. Supporting Bryan was more important than giving in to my social ineptitude.

But even I had my limits. My eyes darted around, looking for the nearest corner I could melt into when I felt a light tap on my shoulder.

"You must be Eli," I heard a man's voice say, almost musically.

I spun around and came face-to-face with a blond man I'd never seen before. "I'm sorry, do I know you?"

"Not even a little bit." He extended his hand to me as a mischievous grin lifted his lips. "I'm Macalister Buchanan, but please feel free to call me Mac."

Mac. Bryan's Mac. "Oh."

I took in his appearance again; he had short blond hair, brown eyes behind thick lashes, was about as tall and fit as Bryan, and had subtle creases around his mouth and eyes, leading me to believe the smile he was flashing me was there more often than not.

"This will be rather embarrassing for me if Bryan hasn't mentioned me as much as he talks about you."

"Oh. No. No, I'm sorry." I extended my hand, which Mac shook, smile never faltering. "Yes, I'm Eli."

"You've done a really great job getting Bryan exposure. He's—how should I put it—rather pleased with you. And your work."

"Thank you. He's worked hard and deserves success." My eyes wandered to the crowd behind us, settling on Bryan. His broad shoulders filled out the white button-up with rolled sleeves that he wore. His eyes locked with mine and he smiled at me for a moment before turning back to his guests. It was only a second or two, but that was all it took for my lips to twist into a grin and for my stomach to feel like I'd been upended. I attributed the strange feeling to my anxiety but couldn't quite pull my eyes away from

Bryan before Mac cleared his throat and raised an eyebrow at me.

Mac scanned me head to foot and back again, sighing in the back of his throat, as if he'd just reached a conclusion about something. "Interesting," he murmured, more to himself than to me. "It's a pleasure to finally meet the guy he's been spending all his spare time with. You certainly are intriguing."

Oh no. Mac probably thought I was some kind of home-wrecker. I didn't want to cause Bryan problems or give him the wrong idea. "No, no. Bryan and I are, uh, just friends. He's mentioned you a lot, and I've been looking forward to meeting you. At some point. I should have expected you'd be here tonight, but the thought really never crossed my mind and—"

Mac snorted a small laugh and lifted his drink to his lips, never taking his eyes off me.

"I'm sorry. I talk too much when I'm nervous."

"Do I make you nervous?"

I shrugged and ran a hand through my hair to occupy my hands. "Yeah, you do. You're Bryan's partner, and I'm making an awful impression."

Mac choked on whatever was in his glass, coughing turning to laughter as he regained his easy composure. "I'm going to have to set you straight there, so to speak. Bryan and I are not dating, nor have we ever been romantically involved. He's not exactly my type. Like, at all. Now, if he had a cute sister…"

Mac kept talking, but I couldn't hear it above the blood pounding in my ears. I felt the flush creeping up my neck and cheeks while my stomach did more aerobics. "You're not… Oh my God. I shouldn't have assumed. I'm so sorry." My eyes fell to the floor as the realization of what I'd just learned sunk in; I was embarrassed that I'd made a fool of myself in front of Mac. More than that, I was actually kind of happy that he and Bryan weren't together. No, happy wasn't right. Relieved, maybe. Whatever it was, it washed over me and was almost strong enough to make me forget that I'd made a horrible misstep with Bryan's best friend.

"Bryan said you worry about things. I'd wager a guess you're doing that right now. It's seriously okay. I'm not offended, and if it'll help, I won't tell Bryan that you thought he and I were boyfriends. Trust me—you wouldn't be the first person to make that leap."

I looked up to see Mac still grinning at me, though not in a condescending or snide way. If he was Bryan's best friend, I should probably put more faith in him to be a decent person, though I couldn't simply shake those feelings I'd become so accustomed to.

"Thank you," I replied quietly, unsure of what else to say. I didn't want Bryan to know about my assumption, but it was a stupid thing to keep from him. Why did it matter? I had no doubts he'd find it amusing and not take offense, yet I still didn't want him to know.

"Don't sweat it, man. Hanging out with you has been putting him in a ridiculously good mood, so maybe I should be thanking you. Care to tell me your secret?" Mac winked at me before finishing his drink.

I make him happy? I bit back a smile and shrugged. "We mostly just watch movies and cook. He started joining me for runs as well."

Mac wrinkled his nose and widened his eyes at me. "*Bryan* running? Shit, I'd love to see that. That guy has the cardio of my dead grandfather."

I burst out laughing, far louder than I probably should have, garnering a few looks from men and women I didn't recognize. I covered my mouth with my hand while my shoulders shook, Mac's own laugh egging me on.

"It's not *that* bad," Bryan's voice said from beside me.

I froze, and my laughter ceased as I turned to him and felt myself shrink. Bryan rested his hand on my shoulder and gave it a firm squeeze while he smiled at me again. It worked to reassure me that he wasn't upset with me, and I found myself leaning into his touch. Based on past experiences, I'd never considered myself to be a very tactile person, but Bryan seemed to bring that out in me. He turned to Mac and they threw playful jabs back and forth before Mac held up his empty drink and excused himself.

"I hope he didn't say anything inappropriate. Mac is a sweetheart, but he's also a perpetual teenager." There was no malice or even a hint of annoyance in Bryan's voice—only the fondness I'd heard before when he talked about Mac; the very same fondness I'd misconstrued for romantic love.

"He was fine—very well-behaved." Bryan stared at me and snorted a laugh. "That's weird to say." I wrinkled my nose and tried again. "He was funny. Seemed nice too. I can see why you like him. He, uh, startled me. He came up behind me and addressed me by name."

"I told him all about you. Most of the people here are our friends, so it probably wasn't difficult to pick you out."

"Yeah, I guess. He'd just have to look for the boring guy who looks like he's about to throw up," I deadpanned.

"Stop. You're not boring. Are you feeling unwell?" Bryan asked, his brows slightly raised in concern.

"No, I'm not sick. I didn't want to let my shortcomings prevent me from supporting you. That"—I flicked my eyes down to my feet then back up to Bryan's—"seemed like a really shitty thing to do for a friend."

"Shit. I didn't think about that. You didn't have to come if you weren't comfortable. I don't want to force you into things you don't want." Bryan clenched his jaw and cast his eyes away from me for a moment. "Don't force yourself to do things you don't want to do for my sake. I'd still consider you a friend if you hadn't come today."

I considered his words and appreciated his concern for me, but he was wrong. "If not for you and Eve, then whom? From what I understand, friends should support each other, even if it's not always easy. For Eve that means standing up with her at her wedding next month, and for you it's me being here today. You're both important to me. I wouldn't be showing that by hiding away at my desk or at home."

Someone called Bryan's name, and we both turned to see a blonde woman waving at him. She was chatting with one of the bloggers I'd invited. Bryan nodded his head and turned back to me, tension faintly visible on his brow.

"I have to go schmooze. You must have hyped me up somethin' fierce for all these people to want to talk to me."

A half grin pulled at my lips, and I shook my head. "Not a chance. You're an easy sell. And your baking speaks for itself; people just needed to come in and try it."

"You flatter me. Are you going back to work this afternoon?"

"No, Andrea told me to take the afternoon and make sure this goes well and that you're happy." As if I needed to be told such a thing.

"I'll be sure to tell her how well you've done. Do you have plans after this since you're off early?" Bryan asked.

"No. I was going to go home and take Prince to the dog park. It's not too far off the trail. It's pretty busy after work, but it's not too bad during the day." We didn't go as often as I'd like, but it was safer for her to go when there were fewer dogs around. Too many owners got spooked when they saw a pit bull, even one as sweet as Prince. I'd hate to have someone complain or do anything to risk losing her.

Bryan's expression softened, his lips forming the faintest of smiles. "Sounds fun. Do you want any company?"

"Sure. You're always welcome to join us, but you don't have plans with your friends tonight?" I motioned to the clusters of people around us. "I'd think you'd want to celebrate."

"That's what we'd be doing. I can only celebrate because of the work you've done for me. Seems fitting to do so with you and that super sweet pup of yours," he said with a smile.

I was beyond thrilled that he wanted to join us. In that moment I forgot about my nerves and could breathe normally, like it was just the two of us in my kitchen or on my couch. "Okay. That would be good."

"I've got another hour that I need to be here. You don't have to stay the entire time, of course, but if you do, feel free to use the kitchen to get away if you need to. No one will go back there except me or maybe Mac if he gets nosy." Bryan ran his fingers over his collar, making sure it was nice and crisp, and checked his sleeves, pleased with how they appeared. "I really do need to go, though."

"Go on. Don't let me keep you any longer. I'll wait here for you—probably in the kitchen," I added quickly.

Bryan laughed softly, dimples on full display, and told me to eat whatever I wanted in the kitchen before drifting off through the small crowds of people. My eyes tracked his every movement until I forced myself to look away. In doing so, I caught sight of Mac watching me from across the room with an amused grin on his face. I waved in response to him winking at me before making my way to the privacy of the kitchen and helping myself to the fare spread about on the stainless-steel counter.

TEN

BRYAN

I WAS JOLTED FROM THE *BEST* DREAM about Eli from the loud, obnoxious sound of "Return of the Mack," signaling that Mac was calling my cell. He insisted on having his own ringtone—and on picking it—and I'd foolishly agreed. That was back in university, so it was too late to complain.

I kept my head buried in my pillow and blindly reached toward the ringing until I found the phone on my night-stand. The friction from my morning wood rubbing against my stomach while I stretched across the bed made me whimper. After the dream I'd had, it wouldn't take long to come. I was already halfway there when I answered the phone and croaked out a husky hello.

"Um, hello? Are you fucking right now?" Mac asked, sounding amused.

"What? No." I flipped onto my back to avoid any more of that agonizing friction. Mac knew me too well not to know exactly what I was doing, and there was no way I could stay horny talking to him. I loved the guy to pieces, and as objectively handsome as he was, he was a serious boner-killer for me.

"Whatever. Are you home?"

"Of course I am," I replied with a groan. My erection was already flagging.

"Is Eli with you?" he asked in that singsong voice that made me want to punch him in the nose most of the time.

I froze. Why would he ask that? Mac knew Eli was straight. "No. Why would he be?"

"Hmm. No reason. Anyway, were you planning on showing up to the game today, or should I stop trying to stall?"

I held the phone away from my face and looked at the time. "Oh, fuck." I shot up and pivoted out of bed in one fluid motion, heading straight for my dresser. "I overslept. I'll be there in twenty. Start without me." I hung up before Mac could reply and dressed in my baseball uniform as quickly as I could. I'd have killed for a shower, but that could wait until after the game. As soon as I finished brushing my teeth, I packed a bag with clean clothes, my phone, and a couple of protein bars, and was out the door.

I plunked down on a bench next to Mac as Axel stepped up to bat. I was sweating and panting from running already, which was a shame, because it was only going to get hotter as the morning went on. I hung my head low and took deep breaths while I promised myself to go running with Eli more to improve my cardio. The loud crack of the bat hitting the ball reached my ears followed by the cheers of our teammates' instructing Axel to haul ass.

Mac nudged my ribs with his elbow and waited until I sat up to speak. "Had a late night, huh?"

"It's not what you think," I said.

Mac ran a gloved hand through his wavy blond hair, messing it up more than anything. "Yeah? What do I think?"

"Don't be coy. It doesn't work for you."

"Don't be obtuse. It makes me look stupid by association," he quipped.

"Obtuse," I muttered.

"It means—"

"I know what it means, dick." I sighed and leaned against his shoulder for support. "I'm tired. We watched two movies last night after going for a run and spending time at the dog park. I got home kinda late and forgot to set my alarm. That's all." I hated that I sounded like I was dismissing my time with Eli, but there really wasn't more to it. Not mutually, anyway. I had such a fun time with him that I honestly did lose track of the time. When *The Last Jedi* ended, I hadn't wanted to leave. Eli sat cross-legged next to me on the couch, and Prince was in my lap—her new favorite place, it seemed—with her head resting on his thigh. His knee lay on top of mine and it was all so… comfortable. Leaving felt wrong, but I couldn't linger around all night without cause. I faked a smile on my way out and told him to have a good night when all I wanted to do was kiss him and hold him until the sun rose.

No wonder I dreamt about him.

"What time did you get home? I was out all night."

"Um, around two."

Mac drew his brows together and sighed. "Eli didn't offer to let you spend the night?"

Um, what? "No. Why would he do that?"

Mac shrugged and turned back to the game. "No reason," he said noncommittally. "Did he sit next to you or at the other end of the couch?" he asked after Santiago struck out.

"He sat next to me."

Mac made an amused sound in his throat but didn't say anything else. For reasons unknown to me, it made me go on the defensive. "It doesn't mean anything. His dog likes me, and she sits in my lap; he likes being close to her."

"*Right*. He likes being close to her," he said dryly. I wasn't sure how to read his tone. It was like he was annoyed with me, yet still somewhat amused. I brushed it off and grunted.

"What did you say to him yesterday?"

"Ah, now that's a secret, and you know how much I love secrets."

I snorted a laugh and shook my head. Yeah, I did know. I also knew he wasn't planning on telling me what they discussed, which was strange. Mac and I told each other everything. He was an expert secret-keeper, but it was usually my secrets he kept from others. Being on the other end of that felt... wrong. What could be so important that he wouldn't want to tell me? Eli had dismissed me when I'd asked him about his chat with Mac as well. Not knowing would probably eat at me, though trying to force it out of Mac would be fruitless, and I'd never even think of threatening the truth out of Eli, whether it was a joke or not.

"Know that we had a lovely chat and I think I got to know him quite well," Mac added with his winning smile.

I sighed in defeat and turned my attention to the game while I stretched my arms and shoulders. The grand opening for Eat Cake was in a week and I couldn't afford to injure myself because I was distracted and sulking. Oh, and we had a game to win, and I'd be damned if I fucked that up.

AFTER WINNING THE GAME, Mac suggested we head to the gym. I'd expected him to try to talk to me about Eli more, but he didn't. He did, however, describe in explicit detail the sex he had with a woman named Jasmyne-with-a-y he met on Tinder the night before. By the time we finished up, I felt like I'd been the one who had sex with her, and my need for a shower had never been stronger. I knew he was upselling the events of the night to distract me, but I didn't call him out on it.

Not having planned on going to the gym after the game, I only had the one change of clean clothes on me, which I'd worn to work out in. I left Mac in the locker room to shower alone and went straight home to avoid having to change into either set of dirty clothes.

The door to the apartment barely closed behind me before I began to rid myself of my clothes. I headed for the shower, not even stopping to pick up after myself. Mac would flip out if my stuff was still scattered about when he got home, but that was at the back of my mind as hot water soaked my hair and shoulders.

The water was a touch too hot, though it wasn't anything my skin wouldn't adjust to in a few moments. I closed my eyes and ran my hands through my hair, immediately feeling better. I exhaled and went about washing my hair and body while my mind drifted off and settled on the very thing I tried most not to think about: Elijah Harper.

He smelled like the ocean after his shower yesterday, and I'd have happily drowned in him if he'd let me. I'd cooked and taken on the stir fry's fragrance, but the ocean scent remained on Eli all evening, subtly mixing with his body's chemistry as the night went on. I wanted that scent to envelop me. I wanted to know he was near without having to open my eyes or rely on touch.

Touch. What would I do if I could touch him? Would I cherish him and lavish him in soft caresses until he cried for more, or would it be frenzied and chaotic—all torrid passion and carnality?

I'd been known to like rough sex from time to time, but I

wanted to feast on Eli. I wanted to slowly draw out every ounce of pleasure he could give then take more until he was left boneless and sated in my arms. I'd kiss his neck and all of those beautiful marks on his fair skin. I wondered if he was covered in them before I remembered that, yes, he was.

The memory of Eli naked and writhing under me had me fully erect in seconds. I couldn't recall a time I'd ever been so fucking hot for someone. It was dizzying—or maybe it was the steam and the fact that it felt like all of the blood in my body was in my cock. I gave myself a quick squeeze at the base, slightly pulling my foreskin back to expose the tip. The shocks of pleasure spread through me, all the way down to my toes. The sensation was heady—too much for me to handle while standing and already unsteady. I shut the water off and went straight for my bed, skipping a towel and kicking my door shut along the way.

I fell on my back and scooted up to rest on my pillows for comfort. I knew I wouldn't last long in the state I was in, but I wanted to enjoy it the best I could. I ran my hand down my chest and stomach until I felt the hair get steadily thicker at the base of my cock. My skin was on fire and it had nothing to do with the near scalding water I'd just stepped out of.

Drawing out the experience was probably what I'd have done if I was thinking clearly, but I wasn't. I wrapped my fingers around my tip and moved my hand up and down, exposing my oversensitive cockhead on every down-stroke. A desperate moan I barely recognized forced its way out of my mouth, urging me to stroke faster.

I closed my eyes, and Eli was everything I could see. Vivid images of him—some imagined and some memories— flooded my mind, invading every thought. I imagined holding his hand while kissing his neck and burying my cock deep inside his taut body, working sighs of pleasure out of him. But it was the image of looking into his eyes and tasting his lips that had me thrusting my hips up into my fist as the mother of all orgasms roared through my body. Cum shot on my chest and stomach as spasm after spasm sent waves of pleasure crashing over me.

My throat was dry from panting and my muscles ached from exertion when I finally melted against the bed. Too sated and weak to move, I lay there and tried to catch my breath as my cum dried all over me. When I was able to, I lifted my head and took in the mess I'd made of myself and sighed; I looked like a damn Toaster Strudel and was in need of another shower.

And perhaps some divine intervention to help me with my Eli dilemma.

I MET with my financial advisor at my father's behest to discuss, well, everything. It was Thursday and the day before the grand opening of Eat Cake, so I was anxious and busy and wanting to be anywhere but at the fucking bank going over my investment portfolio. What got me through those awful two hours was knowing that I was going to see Eli shortly after. It was his idea to open on a Friday in case there were any major problems that needed to be fixed over the weekend. We were concluding our Star Wars movie nights with *Solo*, which I was really excited for. My love for Han hadn't waned while watching Episodes one through three, and I was elated to see him back in *The Force Awakens*.

More than that, I longed to see Eli again. I hadn't seen him in about a week and a half and was ready to crawl out of my skin. We'd been texting nearly every day, but it wasn't the same as seeing him and being able to touch him. I missed the sound of his voice, especially how it sounded thick with sleep. I missed the warmth he exuded whenever he was close to me, and I missed seeing him smile. I fucking missed Prince too. I felt guilty about not dropping by to see her last week, but I'd been so damn busy with finalizing everything for the opening.

I hired a guy to take and fulfill beverage orders after spending more money than I was comfortable with on an industrial coffeemaker. Good coffee was one of the suggestions Eli had been adamant about for patrons who decided to order in. I trusted his judgement implicitly, which is how I ended up with a coffee contraption that set me back almost six grand. However, it did brew some really nice coffee.

"Are you excited about tomorrow?" Eli asked from his seat across the kitchen island. He snacked on the piles of chopped-up carrots, peppers, and halved cherry tomatoes I'd set aside while I julienned some zucchini. At Eli's request, I was making spaghetti primavera again. I couldn't see her from where I stood, but I was certain Prince sat at Eli's feet.

"I am, but I've been thinking about changing the menu. It's way too last minute now, but it's not sitting right with me. Thinking about it kept me up pretty late last night." I conveniently left out that I'd been thinking about Eli even more than the dumb menu, as if I could say that.

Eli swallowed the last cherry tomato he'd popped in his mouth, and I absolutely did not track the movements in his throat when he swallowed it down. His tongue darted out, drawing my attention to his rosy pink lips. He licked his bottom lip in what was probably an innocent gesture, but my dick had other ideas and twitched at the sight. I'd stopped chopping veggies and was halfway down the rabbit hole when Eli's voice pulled me back.

"You're just nervous. I've tasted everything you'll be

putting out, and, while I'm no expert, it was all delicious. Like, the best desserts I've ever had. I watched you revise that menu so many times until you were happy with it. My research showed that you should leave it as is for at least two months until you have regular patrons. Adding a weekly or even daily special item will be exciting enough in the beginning before you make any significa—" Eli cut himself off and stared at me with his perfect brown eyes. "I-I mean it's your business, and you can do whatever you want with it. I didn't mean to sound like I was telling you what to do." His shoulders slumped, like they used to when he'd embarrassed himself, and he dropped his gaze from mine. I hadn't seen that type of reaction from him in weeks and it made me want to jump over the counter and hug him.

I set down the knife and wiped my hands on a dish towel while I spoke. "It's all right. I know what you meant. And you're right. I'm nervous and freaking out. Everything is as close to perfect as it's going to be, and I need to relax."

Eli looked up at me, and I was relieved to see a crooked grin on his face. "Take it from me, it's easier said than done."

I huffed in amusement then resumed my work with the knife. I wanted to ask Eli more about his anxiety, but no time seemed to be the right time. He'd just mentioned it offhandedly, so I tried to casually probe. "Have you always been, um—"

"Batshit crazy," Eli muttered nonchalantly.

"Not what I was going to say."

"Sorry. I'm being an asshole. You're wondering if I have a diagnosis for my anxiety and stuff? The answer is no. I've always been a bit antisocial. It got so much worse after my mom died." His voice was even, very matter-of-fact, though his movements were twitchy. He was clearly uncomfortable but was telling me anyway.

"Shit. I'm sorry."

"It's okay. I mean, it's not okay, but it was a long time ago. I became a bit of a recluse after she died. Working at Red Right Hand has helped with that, though. Eve has especially helped me."

I dropped my head and smiled. I really wanted to meet her. I couldn't exactly thank her for looking after Eli, but I wanted to. Thinking about how alone he must have been made my heart ache, but I couldn't dwell on what I couldn't change. I had to focus on what I could affect, and that meant being the best friend I could be.

"You've really helped me too, you know," Eli said in a hushed voice, meeting my eyes, though submitting nonetheless with his body language. "Not to sound weird or strange, you're very important to me. Maybe it's because you're a guy—I don't know. It's different than it is with Eve. She looks out for me, makes sure I'm taking care of myself in an almost motherly way. With you…" Eli trailed off, shifting on his stool. I wanted to tell him that he was damn important to me too, but I knew he had more to say, and I longed to hear it. "I'm not sure how to describe what it feels like with you. You're the first real guy friend I've had in my adult life, and I just don't know what that's supposed to look like." He rubbed the back of his neck and huffed a bitter laugh. "I'm probably saying too much. Guys don't really do that with each other from what I've observed, huh? I don't mean to make you uncomfortable or anything; I just want you to know that your friendship means a lot to me. I mean, you do too—mean a lot to me, that is. Okay, I'm going to shut up now."

Speechless. It'd only happened a few times in my life, but Eli had rendered me speechless. Moments before I'd had a hundred things I wanted to say to him. Now, after hearing Eli speak so candidly, all of my thoughts left me. I blinked at him, no doubt looking like a fool, while I processed his words. Cinnamon-and-caramel irises conveying such trust and vulnerability pinned me, making it harder to focus.

Too long had gone by with my silence hanging between us. There wasn't anything I could say that would accurately express what I was feeling—save for impulsively telling him that I was falling in love with him, which was off the table. I dropped the knife and rounded the island until I stood beside Eli. His forehead crinkled, probably in confusion, as he slid off the stool toward me. He parted his lips, but I grabbed the front of his shirt before he could get any words out, and pulled him against my chest. I wrapped my arms around his back and hoped that hugging him would tell him everything I couldn't say.

I knew I'd shocked him, and I probably should have asked him if the contact was okay, but I wasn't thinking about anything other than letting him know he was loved. He froze when I first embraced him, but not two seconds later, his arms wrapped around me and his hands fisted my T-shirt. A deep, relieved sigh rushed out of me, and I turned my head to murmur in his ear.

"Thank you." I pulled back and released him before continuing. "I feel very much the same about you. I've had plenty of male friends, yet I've never known anyone like you. Having you in my life has made me a better person, and I can't thank you enough for that."

"I don't know, you were pretty great from the start," Eli said with a small grin.

"And now I'm better. Oh my, do you think I'm perfect now?" I joked, eliciting a full smile from Eli.

Scarlet crept up Eli's neck, and his Adam's apple bobbed as he swallowed. "If ever there was a perfect person, I have no doubt it would be you."

Kiss him. That was the prevailing thought in my mind. Consequences be damned, just kiss him. I didn't need to remind myself why I couldn't. In my mind and in my heart there were no consequences. In reality, I knew that I could destroy everything between us by giving into my base desires, and after the progress we just made, I would not allow that to happen.

"You're too nice to me. You'll give me a complex if that continues and then I'll be a *real* nightmare." I forced a smile and lightly nudged Eli's upper arm. "Hey, and don't worry so much about us. There's no one right way to be friends with someone. This"—I motioned between us—"is working well for us both—that's all that matters." I flashed a smile when Eli nodded and then went back around to the cutting board to resume prepping our dinner.

ELEVEN

ELI

I'D ALMOST THROWN UP WHEN I told Bryan how I felt
about him. And I'd told him about my mom—more
than I'd even told Eve. I didn't know what came over me last
night, but saying it all felt right. Sitting at my desk the next
morning, I had no regrets. It wasn't easy to say, and I was
glad I didn't fuck it up, like I'd done with so many other
things in my life.

I sent Bryan a text wishing him good luck when I woke
up. He'd replied immediately and said he just put red
velvet cupcakes in the oven. I promised him I'd stop in
during my lunch break and see how things were going,
which seemed to please him. I wanted to go earlier, but I
had other files to work on, including a brand-new one for a
tech start-up. Something to do with creating phone apps. I
really wasn't sure what it was all about, hence why I needed
to log some desk time and get acquainted with my new
clients' venture.

I also had a couple of emails and calls from Hana to
return, which I didn't tell Eve about to avoid her teasing. I
knew Hana liked me; I just tried not to think about it. It was

the same tactic I'd been using to avoid difficult things my entire life, even before I lost my mom.

As much as I didn't seek out relationships, women always seemed to be drawn to me—until they figured out that I couldn't love them. Hana was being more persistent than most, and I wasn't sure how I should handle that.

"You look like you need help," Eve said. I looked up to see her leaned around her computer with a knowing smile spanning her red lips.

"It's Hana. She's been calling and emailing me for weeks. I don't want to be rude, but she won't leave me alone." I knew I was whining—I didn't care. Dealing with Hana was at the bottom of my list of priorities.

"Oh, I'm well aware. She emailed me asking for your whereabouts just this mornin'."

I groaned and dropped my head to my desk. "Ugh. You were right."

"I always am, pet. Now scoot over." Eve rolled her chair around the desk and bumped into mine when I didn't move fast enough. "We're gun'na send 'er a strongly worded reply." She accentuated her accent, making me smile.

Eve winked at me then her fingers tapped away at my keyboard, far more eloquently than I ever could have mustered. While continuing to type, she glanced at me with a raised eyebrow and asked if I found a date for her wedding. The big day was quickly approaching at just three weeks away.

Honestly, I'd forgotten all about finding a date. Bryan had taken up all of my non-work-related thoughts since we reconnected. Posed with the question, he was the only person I thought to take. No. He was the only person I *wanted* to take. Eve had several cousins that could accompany me in the event that I didn't find a date, but, if Bryan was willing, that measure wouldn't be necessary.

"I was thinking I'd ask Bryan if he wanted to go with me. He wants to meet you." I looked down at Eve's stilled fingers and shrugged. "I'm not sure he'll say yes, though."

Eve turned toward me and brushed my hair behind my ear. "Why wouldn't he?"

I shrugged again. "I don't know."

"Yes, you do. Tell me what's buggin' ya."

Of course she knew. I did too, but I was scared to say it —scared to put the words out there and give them traction. But I'd been doing a lot of new things that scared me in the past. I could do one more.

I leaned in toward Eve and spoke quietly to avoid eavesdroppers—and because it was the most I could manage. "I'm worried that he won't want to see me anymore. I mean, now that our working relationship is over and we don't have any movies left to watch. What if he was only indulging me to make working with me easier instead of awkward and stilted, like it was in the beginning?"

"You don't really believe that, do you?" she asked.

"I… no. No, I don't. I know—I *know* he wouldn't do that. Yet there's a part of me that keeps whispering that dreaded 'what if.' It's followed me around for my entire life and has kept me back from so much. I thought I was keeping myself safe. 'What if they laugh at you?' 'What if you fail?' I've asked myself questions like that ever since I can remember. I'm used to it now, but with Bryan it's so much worse." I swallowed and licked my lips, which felt dry beyond measure. "What if I lose him? I don't know what I'd do."

Eve pulled me into a hug, stroking the back of my hair. That was twice in as many days that I had someone hug me —more than in the last two years. "You won't lose anything unless you don't communicate. It's the same in all types of relationships. You have to talk to him. Just ask him. No is always a possibility, but isn't the chance of him saying yes worth the risk?"

"Of course it is."

"Ask him today. Oh, don't look at me like that—I know good and well you're plannin' on going down there to see him at some point today. Ask him then. Don't waste time and let yourself get worked up and stuck in downward spiraling thoughts."

"You're right. You always are. I'll try to ask him at lunch."

"Better get going. Your reply to Hana was sent a few minutes ago. I don't think she'll bother you anymore."

I thanked Eve, grabbed my phone and bag, and headed out to go see how Bryan was doing.

Busy. That was how Bryan was. Lunchtime turned out to be a bad time to drop in if I wanted to talk to him. He still came out and greeted me, but he couldn't stay long. Despite his smile he had bags under his eyes, magnified by his glasses, and looked like he needed three days of sleep to catch up.

"Have you eaten today?" I asked.

"I had a couple brownies this morning from the first batch," he replied around a yawn.

I frowned at him then reached into my bag and pulled out a container of leftover pasta. "Here"—I pushed it against his chest, forcing him to grab it—"go back there and eat this so you don't drop."

Bryan looked down at the container then back up at me. "What about you? I don't want to eat your lunch."

"I'll pick something up on my way back to the office. I'll pass by a hundred different places to pick from; you're stuck here for a few more hours. Eat." I didn't care that I sounded bossy. He needed to take a break, even if the place was busy.

I wasn't all that surprised to see such a big turnout. The lunch crowd in the area was massive and Paige Turner wrote a raving article about Eat Cake. The other bloggers did too, generating a lot of positive exposure. I was so happy for Bryan, even if it meant my time with him was cut short. Not wanting to keep him monopolized, I excused myself and said I'd be back after close to meet up.

"Busy day, huh?" I stated the obvious, but I needed an icebreaker to work up to inviting Bryan to the wedding. I sat on a stool in front of Bryan while he stood and rubbed the back of his neck.

"Fuuuuuuck. I underestimated how busy I'd be. Don't get me wrong, it's fantastic and I hope it holds up, but I'm exhausted."

I slid off the stool he'd offered me when I arrived and slid it toward him. "Sit. You've probably been on your feet all day."

"Thanks," he said as he sat down with a groan that spoke of sore, tired muscles. He took his glasses off and set them on the counter before rubbing his bloodshot eyes.

I rubbed my palms together as my eyes danced around the room. All of the cleaning was finished, and the kitchen was just as pristine as it had been after installation. My gaze lingered on the wall I'd helped paint and I smiled to myself. There was no way everything between Bryan and me had been fake or one-sided. So, why was I still so nervous to ask him? Every time I tried to speak it felt like my throat constricted. Even looking directly at him made me feel fuzzy and strange.

My inability to effectively communicate frustrated me to no end. I felt paralyzed in my own body as I helplessly screamed at myself to act. I knew my anxiety was bad—I never noticed just how crippling it could be.

What felt like hours of struggling for me were probably only seconds for Bryan. He always picked up on my mood changes, but he seemed off today too. I chalked it up to him being tired and stressed all day, though I'd never seen him quite so drained.

"Hey, ah, I'm having another baseball game on Sunday morning. If you want to come play with us, you're more than welcome," he said suddenly, sounding uncharacteristically uncertain—sounding like me.

"I-I'd love to come, but I don't think I'd want to play. Would watching the game be okay?"

"That depends. Are you going to cheer for me? I'll expect a sign—maybe even pom-poms," Bryan teased with a smirk.

I snorted, and covered my nose and mouth with my hands. It wasn't an intentional, amused snort; I snorted like a tickled pig rolling in shit and was mortified.

Bryan tried not to, but his face cracked and he burst out laughing. Seeing him smile again made me do the same, and my shame and anxiety melted away. How he was able to consistently improve my moods, I didn't know, though I was so appreciative of it. Just a look or smile from him was all it took to pull me out of the depths of my pessimism.

"I don't think I'd look good in a skirt, but I'd love to cheer for you. Unless that's not something people do with baseball. I've never actually been to a game," I admitted.

"You can cheer if you want to. Just you being there will be enough for me. And for the record, with your legs, I think you could totally pull off a skirt." He winked at me and we both laughed, dissolving the last bit of hesitation in me.

Once we calmed down and a comfortable silence fell over us, I licked my lips and spoke. "I have something I'd like to invite you to as well. Eve is getting married in three weeks and I was hoping you wouldn't mind going with me. I get a plus one, and she told me I had to bring someone, which was probably her way of forcing me to meet a new girl come to think of it. Anyway, that's not really important right now." I somehow managed to keep my eyes on Bryan and not look away, although the urge to do so tugged at me.

Bryan tilted his head and a half grin producing one dimple tugged at his lips. "You want me to be your date?"

"I—uh, I suppose I do. No, I definitely do. There's no one else I'd rather take. I mean, even if I had a lot of options, you'd still be my first choice. Shit. I'm going to stop talking now."

"I'd love to go with you," Bryan said evenly. "Is that why you were nervous when you came in?"

I sighed and nodded. "Yes."

"You didn't actually think I'd say no, did you?"

"I'm dumb, I know."

"You're anything but." Bryan scanned the kitchen and huffed, rising to his feet. "Wanna grab some tacos and beer and go back to your place? I'm too tired to cook tonight and puppy kisses always give me life."

Of course I said yes to that. That was a perfect evening if ever I heard one. Then again, everything about Bryan was perfect.

The game was really exciting to watch. Bryan's team won and as much as I wanted to scream and cheer, I couldn't allow myself to do so. The thought of drawing that much attention to myself in public made me nauseous. I did wave at Bryan when it was his turn to bat. He smiled and tipped his hat at me before raising the bat and adjusting his grip. He missed the first ball but nailed the second in what I guess was a home run.

Seeing him in action made me understand his physique more. His broad shoulders and strong arms were conditioned for the sport. The guys on the team who hit the ball the farthest all looked to be more buff than the others, yet those other guys were faster. From what I observed, other than a few sprints to bases, there wasn't a whole lot of running involved, which explained why he'd nearly died on our first few runs together.

I'd seen it a lot on TV and in movies, but I hadn't realized that ass-slapping was such a huge part of real-life sports. I first noticed it when Mac did it to Bryan, then I observed most of the players engaging. I'd never thought about another man's ass, but I'd also never played organized sports, so who knew. All of the attention to butts made me notice that Bryan had a pretty nice one, if I had to judge. His whole body was something I aspired to when I was a teen: strong and undeniably masculine.

I couldn't picture my present self like that, but it sure worked for Bryan. He had so much raw energy and strength, yet he was the sweetest guy who liked baby-talking to dogs and baking sweets with the utmost care. I had to smile just thinking about it.

After the game I was introduced to the guys on the team and got to talk to Mac again. He was all smiles and charisma again, and I wondered if he was ever "off." His blond hair shone bright in the midmorning sun, such a stark contrast to Bryan's black hair.

Mac slung his arm over my shoulders and invited me to grab a drink and lunch with the guys who were going out to celebrate. One glance at Bryan coming our way with a dimpled smile on his face had me saying yes before I could even think about it.

THE NEXT FEW weeks leading up to the wedding were some of the busiest of my life. I ended up helping Eve with most last-minute preparations since I saw her for eight hours a day and it was all so much. I never thought I would get married, and all of the drama surrounding Eve's wedding helped reaffirm that for me.

Bryan helped me choose a suit, opting for suspenders, no jacket, and bow tie that matched the bridesmaids' turquoise dresses. He had to call Mac for help on the shoes, claiming he was strictly a sneakers and boots kind of guy.

The rehearsal dinner went well, and I wasn't too overwhelmed by it before I remembered we'd be on display in front of one hundred guests during the real deal. They wouldn't be focused on me, but the "what if" demon in me had its day without Bryan or Eve around to talk some sense into me.

That evening, I attended Eve's bachelorette party. It was one of those moments where I was doing it for her as a show of support, because God knows I wanted to lock myself in a room alone and wait until everyone left.

Drinking with Bryan's friends had been largely relaxed and comfortable. Eve's all-female bachelorette party was, in a word, wild. I'd always gotten along better with women, but I'd never seen them quite like they were that night. Mob mentality swept through them and it only intensified when the male stripper showed up dressed as a police officer.

The black-haired man was a talented dancer and, uh, pretty *gifted* if the bulge in his thong wasn't artificial. While all of the other attendees screamed and said some things that made me blush, all I did was sit and compare the guy to Bryan. Perhaps it was that they both had impossibly black hair that I felt the need to do such a comparison, or maybe I was bored. Either way, the stripper didn't have any advantages over Bryan aside from being taller, which seemed inconsequential. Put simply, I thought Bryan was attractive whereas Officer Dick did nothing for me.

Does that mean Bryan does something for me? Well, yes. Kind of. He did a lot for me. He nearly choked to death laughing when I told him about the stripper. I omitted that I thought he was better looking, but I wasn't sure why.

On nights I wasn't with Bryan or Eve, I dabbled in inking some abstracts on the remaining cardstock I had from when I did Bryan's logo. I kept it to myself in case I didn't stick with it, but as time went on, I found more enjoyment in the solitary act. When I ran out of cardstock I bought more and even browsed canvases. I still wasn't ready for that, but I felt like I might actually get there again.

The day of the wedding finally came. I was such a nervous wreck that Bryan had to tie my bow tie for me on the car ride to the venue. Neither Eve nor Samir were overly religious and opted to have the ceremony in a botanical garden and the reception inside a Victorian banquet hall adorned in white, teal, and gold.

After we arrived, I was whisked away to fulfill my bridesman duties and didn't see Bryan again until I walked out arm in arm with Samir's lone groomswoman and took my place on Eve's side of the altar. I was kept busy and hadn't the free time to dwell on missing Bryan, but as I stood beside the rest of the bridal party and looked around at the full rows of guests, I realized how badly I wanted to see him.

I found him instantly, seated in the second row next to Eve's spirited younger brother. He wore a light green dress shirt that apparently went well with the turquoise bow tie I wore. It also made Bryan's pale green eyes pop more than they already did.

I focused on Eve and Samir during their vows, then my eyes wandered back to Bryan when the priest spoke again. By the time the "I do's" were exchanged and everyone clapped and cheered, Bryan was looking back at me with a smile.

TWELVE

BRYAN

THE BRIDE AND GROOM WERE ALL smiles as they greeted the applauding crowd as husband and wife. I missed the first kiss because I couldn't take my eyes off Eli standing up there. When he looked back at me my heart lurched in my chest. It was almost as if he needed to see me as much as I needed him. I couldn't help but smile at the thought.

"Is it socially acceptable for me to get drunk now?" Dubhlainn asked from beside me at our table inside the reception hall. He was Eve's eighteen-year-old brother. His hair was the same shade of red as hers, but much longer by the look of it. He had it tied back in a loose bun for convenience more than fashion. I hadn't had a chance to meet Eve yet, though they seemed alike based on what Eli told me about her: wildly outspoken and bold.

"Wait until after they have their first dance. And perhaps until you're twenty-one."

"Legal drinking age in Ireland is eighteen," he snapped back. "Besides, I have a false ID."

I snorted and shook my head. "You're trouble, but I won't rat on you."

"Yes. Aoibheann knows better than to seat me with our parents," he replied with a lazy grin. I supposed he was right, considered both sets of parents were at the table closest to the wedding cake. We sat at the next closest table with people I'd been told were cousins.

The bridesmaids and groomsmen strolled inside arm in arm and sat down up on a raised platform with a long table adorned in white cloth. Eve and Samir made their grand entrance shortly after and danced to a Gaelic ballad I was unfamiliar with while everyone looked on with happy faces. For a second, I imagined what it would be like to slow dance with Eli in front of all these people. To hold him flush against me while we swayed to a ballad that perfectly articulated everything I wanted to say to him.

Before I got too caught up in the thought, the DJ played an up-tempo song and the rest of the bridesmaids and groomsmen took to the dance floor. Except for Eli. He came straight over to me. The poor guy looked drained, so I offered him my chair, which he accepted with thanks.

He greeted Dubhlainn before the younger man excused himself to go "get a gargle," which I assumed meant a drink.

"You look exhausted," I said, taking the now empty seat next to Eli.

"I am. I've been going nonstop since arriving, but it's over now," he huffed.

As I opened my mouth to reply, one of the bridesmaids waltzed over with a big smile stretching her red-painted lips. My heart sank when she asked him to do the one thing I wanted most in that moment but couldn't have; she asked him to dance.

"Thank you for the offer, Addy, but I can't. That would

be extremely rude to my date," he said as he motioned to me, leaving me just as dumbstruck as poor Addy.

"O-oh. I didn't… sorry. Have a good evening, Elijah." She darted away toward three waiting women, whispering to them. Their surprised reactions confirmed what I'd expected.

"Do you know what you just told her?" I asked Eli. "She thinks you're gay now."

Without missing a beat, Eli turned to me and shrugged. "And what's wrong with that?"

"Well, nothing."

"I'm far too tired, but if I was going to dance with anyone other than Eve tonight, it would be you." He said it so matter-of-fact, as if it was the most obvious answer. "They can think whatever they want about me, especially if it means they'll leave me alone."

Well, damn. I shouldn't have been surprised, but there I was, staring at Eli like he had three heads. Finally, I laughed —it was all I could do. "I love the way your mind works."

He leaned against my shoulder and groaned as a reply, making me giggle. "Come on. Let's grab some drinks before dinner is served. Maybe you can show me around the garden before it gets dark." Eli yawned and nodded. He was reluctant to stand back up, though once we exited the banquet hall and ventured into a less densely populated area he began to come back to life.

With full champagne flutes in hand, we wandered around the garden, taking in all the different colors and savoring the sweet scent of each offering. We worked our way to a gazebo overlooking a pond at the back of the garden and sat down on a bench to watch the sunset. Neither of us spoke as we sipped our drinks and took in the sight, but the moment was almost better without words.

Eli yawned and rested his head against my shoulder as he'd grown accustomed to doing when we watched movies late at night. His breathing slowed, and I realized he was actually falling asleep.

"Elijah," I whispered. "You're going to hurt your neck if you fall asleep like that." A sleepy moan came as a reply. I hesitated for a moment before I carefully pulled my arm out from between us and shifted Eli so his head rested on my chest. As much as I wanted to, I didn't dare wrap my arm around his back and rested it against the back of the bench instead.

The sun had gone down entirely, and string lanterns shimmered in the darkened space while lanterns illuminated the path behind us. The sound of the thriving reception was distant to my ears, second to the steady inhale and exhale of Eli's breathing. I whispered his name again and got no reaction. Unable to resist the urge, I leaned my head down and smelled his hair, groaning in my throat at the scent that was so distinctly Eli, only much stronger this close. I didn't trust myself to do it again and instead focused my attention on the stillness of the dark water, the sounds of the frogs in it, and the warmth radiating from Eli.

"I thought I might find you fellas out here," an accented voice said quietly.

I flinched at the unexpected voice, and turned to see Eve standing next to me. She'd changed into a green-and-white dress—perhaps a nod to both her Irish roots and Samir's Arab lineage—and was eyeing me closely with a faint smile.

"Sorry for ducking out. I figured Eli could use a break, but he kind of fell asleep."

"No apology necessary. I was coming out to check on him. I see you've got it handled." She lifted her chin and motioned to Eli, who was still lying on my chest.

"I'm Bryan, by the way," I said, offering her my left hand, which she shook.

"Aoibheann—but call me Eve, everyone does. I've heard a

lot about ya. Only good things, but I wanted to see for myself."

Her tone was friendly yet pointed. It was clear to me that she wasn't happy having gone these months without knowing who Eli was spending his time with. I loved that she was so concerned over his well-being. "I've heard a lot about you too. Do I pass your test?" I asked with a raised eyebrow and a knowing grin.

She hummed and took a few steps to stand in front of Eli. She knelt down and brushed his hair behind his ear then stood up and faced me. "If ya were an arsehole I'd have had you thrown out earlier."

"Dubhlainn," I muttered. "You sent a spy."

"Handsome and smart. My, my."

We both snickered before she excused herself to head back to her celebration. I remained on the bench with Eli, lightly twitching in his sleep. I'd eventually wake him up so he wouldn't miss the entire party, but I was content to self-ishly enjoy the moment for just a bit longer.

ELI STARTED COMING to watch my games regularly in the weeks that followed the wedding. Had I known he'd want to, I'd have asked him long ago, but it was happening now and that was what mattered. I talked to the team and got the go-ahead to schedule our future games closer to Eli so he could bring Prince too. When I told him the good news, he hugged me after half a second's hesitation. Progress.

Prince was a big hit with the guys and served as a bridge for them to get to know Eli more. He was modest and uncomfortable talking about himself, yet he was a different person when he talked about Prince, and all of the guys could see it. The love he had for that dog was so palpable, I couldn't for the life of me understand why he thought he was unable to love. Anyone who had ever said such an awful thing to him clearly didn't understand him or the impact it would have on a person like him. He had a lot of love in him —it just didn't always manifest in obvious ways, like it might in most people. His love for Prince was pure and unguarded. I was sure he loved Eve and me in some capacity, but that was completely different and, at least in my case, a slow process. We grew closer with every passing day and when I looked at him now, I could clearly see that I mattered to him in some way.

With Prince, it was a lot more obvious. When she saw me at games she went *crazy*. The way she greeted me at Eli's apartment was nothing compared to when we were out in open spaces. Eli would unhook her leash and she'd dart toward me and jump into my arms, tail wagging nonstop. She really was the sweetest dog.

On the days Eli brought her, we went to places with patios for our postgame drinks. Axel's sister had a rottweiler, which he started bringing to games and play dates for Prince after learning how much she liked other people and animals. The two dogs got along extremely well and would run around for hours if left to their own devices—it was absolutely adorable.

Eli still took her for runs every day, even if we had a game near a dog park or she had a play date. I always joined him for evening runs after games and beer, even though I felt like a bag of ass. I *did* end up hurling once, much to my chagrin. Running with Eli was great—because any time spent with him was—but my favorite thing to do with him was curl up on the couch and watch movies.

A couple of weeks later, Eli asked Mac and me if we wanted to have dinner with Eve and Samir. We decided on

Korean barbecue because it seemed like a good way for everyone to get acquainted without the pomp and circumstance of a structured sit-down meal. And Mac had *begged*.

Mac spent the night away from the apartment, and had arrived ahead of Eli and me. He was pacing when we approached him at the restaurant's entrance, and I groaned. That bastard only paced when he fucked up.

"What did you do?" I ground out. Eli tilted his head and frowned, probably confused by my sudden sharp and short tone.

"Now, listen. I didn't know what Eve looked like, and—"

"You did *not* hit on Eve." I groaned again. Mac smirked and shrugged while Eli's eyes went wide and his mouth fell open before curving into a grin.

"In my defense, I did not know she was hot. Neither of you bastards told me she was a knock-out redhead. You"—he pointed at me—"especially know I'm weak for redheaded women!" Mac whisper-shouted and flailed his hands for emphasis.

"Where was Sam?" Eli asked, giggling adorably next to me.

"Parking the car apparently. She shut me down before he came inside. Maybe she won't tell him?" Mac asked Eli hopefully.

Eli shook his head. "No, she definitely will. But don't worry. Sam won't care… much."

Mac sighed and pushed up the sleeves on his lightweight beige sweater. We went inside and were led to a round table with Eve and Samir whispering and snickering. When they caught sight of Mac, the snickers turned into shit-eating grins. For once in his life, Mac had nothing to say and plunked down in a chair next to Samir. Eli sat by Eve, and I took the spot between him and Mac.

A server came by with water for the table, and Mac stood

when they left. "All right. Let's get this shit cleared. Hi." Mac waved at Samir. "I'm Mac, and I have a thing for beautiful red-haired women. As I'm sure you've heard, I hit on your wife—congratulations, by the way—about ten minutes ago. I just wanted to apologize so we can all acknowledge and move past my prior transgression." He sat back down and downed his water with a frown. "Goddamn, let's get some drinks going, guys. This is a celebration."

Mac's antics were met with laughter, and proper intro-ductions were made. For the first time since we'd been in public together, Eli wasn't nervous in a crowd. He'd started coming over to my place, with Prince, for some game nights a few weeks ago, and I loved that he and Mac got along so well. Seeing that carry over in an uncontrolled setting caused me to beam with pride for Eli. He'd come a long way from the man he was when I first walked into that boardroom at Red Right Hand, and I was thrilled to be a part of the change in him.

The rest of the dinner went on without any friction. Samir and Eve were good, kind people and weren't easily offended by Mac's… Mac-ness. Everyone ate and drank too much, save for Samir, who wasn't a big drinker. We parted ways with a promise to meet up again soon, and I waved as the silver Camry with Samir, Eve, and Eli pulled away.

"Are you drowning yet?" Mac asked me.

"What?"

"Four months ago, I told you to be careful and not get in over your head. You've been doing a pretty shitty job at not falling in love with him," Mac said after nudging me with his elbow.

I sighed and brushed my hand through my hair, tugging at my nape. "I don't know what to do. I want him more than I've ever wanted anything or anyone in my life, and that scares me. I can't stop, but I can never have him."

Mac slung his arm over my shoulders and pulled me into a hug. "I know, Bry. Come on. Let's go home." We broke apart, though he kept his arm over my shoulders as we walked home on a breezy October evening.

Mac smugly dropped his cards on the table and exclaimed, "Aces up, bitches!"

Eli and I whined and moaned as we handed over the last of our chips for the third game in a row. Eli banged his head on the table while I sat back in my chair and crossed my arms. "I swear you have to be cheating. This shit has been going on for years."

"Years?" Eli asked, lifting his head. "You've been losing to him for that long?"

"He sure has. If you hadn't noticed, our dear Bryan is a glutton for punishment. Oh yes, he's quite the masochist," Mac replied with a wink.

"Fuck you," I said with a half grin. "I don't always lose. And I'm not a masochist."

"That's debatable," Mac mumbled before he turned to Eli. "Do you have Halloween plans?"

Eli looked to me then shook his head at Mac.

"Good! My birthday is on the thirty-first, and I'd love to see you there."

"Okay." Eli's smile did nothing to calm the urge I had to lean across the table and kiss him until we both couldn't breathe. "Thank you for inviting me."

Mac waved his hand, a blue poker chip wedged between his middle and index finger. "Don't be silly; of course you're invited. Unfortunately, you"—Mac looked under the table where Prince was lying—"can't come to Oasis with us."

"What's Oasis?" Eli asked. He took a long pull on his beer, finishing it.

"Ah, it's the new gay club that opened on Halstead a

couple months ago." Mac got up and ran to fetch three more bottles for us.

"Thanks. Um, why would you want to celebrate at a gay bar?" I didn't miss the flush coloring the tips of Eli's ears.

Mac snorted. "Oh, easy. Do you have any idea how many straight women go to gay bars? I always score when we go out." Mac nodded to me. "Bry really is the best wingman."

Eli opened his new beer with unsteady hands and rolled his eyes. "I can't believe I ever thought you two were a couple."

"Wait, what?" I blurted out. Eli thought Mac and I were together? When? Why didn't he ask me? Mac's wandering eyes told me he already knew and then it clicked. This was what they were both keeping from me—what they discussed at the launch.

"Um, yeah. I mistakenly assumed Mac was your… It was an assumption I shouldn't have made."

I didn't know how to take that. I sat there, blinking stupidly at Eli with nothing to say. Mac must have noticed my lack of brain function and intervened.

"''Twas a good time. Awkward. Endearing. Anyway, my birthday is on Halloween, so—and this goes for both of you—don't even think about showing up without costumes. Bry, it's your turn to deal."

THIRTEEN

ELI

BRYAN HELPED ME PICK A COSTUME a week before Halloween, which was quite the affair. I hadn't gone out for Halloween since I was young enough to trick or treat holding my mom's hand; costumes had evolved so much since then. We spent an hour browsing with no luck when Bryan asked if I wanted to pick his costume.

Bryan was easy to shop for. I thought about what would look good on him and nearly everything applied. Then I thought about what would be special for us—er, for him— and the answer became clear. I picked out a Han Solo costume for him and flushed when he tried it on. I couldn't explain why, but seeing him model the costume with a tentative smile on his face made me feel… warm in a way I hadn't felt before. My body prickled, and every inch of my skin felt like it was on fire. Perhaps it was the crowd and my desire to take Bryan and go home to my quiet, familiar space.

Bryan asked me how he looked, and I gave him an honest answer and said he was more handsome than young Harrison Ford, which made him blush. He changed, and we continued searching for me with no luck. I had no idea what

I wanted and the idea of wearing anything other than my normal clothes made me sweat.

Bryan finally stopped me and asked if I trusted him to choose for me. I thought about it for a moment and nodded, then he led me over to the changing rooms and sat me down on a stool inside one. He told me to take a few moments to myself and wait for him to come back with my costume. So I did just that.

I could still hear the voices of other people around me, but being isolated from the crowd did wonders for calming me down. *Leave it to Bryan to know I needed a break and take over.* It astounded me that he knew me better than I knew myself sometimes. He never missed any of my shifting moods or quirks and found them all to be perfectly acceptable, never making me feel like I was abnormal for needing… anything. It didn't matter what the circumstance was, Bryan was always patient and supportive, but also knew when I could be pushed to try new things. He was simply incredible.

A light knock on the door pulled me out of my thoughts and I called out, asking who was there.

"It's just me," Bryan's voice returned.

I got up and unlocked the door for him, and he stepped into the tight space, closing the door behind him. One of his arms was behind his back and he looked so eager to show me what he was hiding.

"Feeling better now?" he asked.

"Yes, much better. Thanks," I said quietly.

"You can tell me when you need a break—always. I won't ever get mad or anything." I nodded, unable to speak around my constricting throat. It made me squirrelly when he was so sweet to me. Having such kind things be said to me regularly was still so new. I imagined it might make me uncomfortable had the words come from anyone else, but I loved hearing them from Bryan.

"If you absolutely hate what I picked, I won't make you wear it." He pulled his arm out from behind his back, revealing a baseball uniform in a bag.

"Baseball?" I asked.

"Indeed. Chicago Cubs—they're my team."

"You mean they're your favorite?"

"Yes," he answered.

"I'll buy it." The idea of wearing something that would make Bryan happy made me feel warm again. I wanted to make him happy more than I realized, and if wearing this costume was a start, I'd do it.

I tried on the uniform, and Bryan seemed to like it. He made a kind of strangled noise in his throat when I stepped out of the changing room, which I guess was a good thing. We rang up our costumes then went for lunch before going shopping for shoes and the finishing touches to complete the looks.

WE LEFT from Mac and Bryan's apartment with another of their friends I hadn't met before. Her name was Blake and she was very friendly and intrigued by me, or so she said. She mistook me for Bryan's boyfriend when we were first introduced, but he was quick to correct her. I wondered if Bryan had a boyfriend—no, he couldn't. He spent all of his time at work, with Mac, or with me.

It was selfish of me, but I was glad he didn't have a boyfriend. I didn't consider myself a jealous person by nature —and I wasn't remotely jealous of the deep friendship Bryan and Mac had—yet the thought of a nonexistent boyfriend had me wanting to lay a claim on him that I didn't have any right to lay. Those feelings intensified when he came out of his room in his full costume and some eyeliner Blake had insisted would "add some drama." I couldn't deny that it looked great on him.

Mac had booked a booth at Oasis with bottle service, and thank God for it. I probably would have died if not for the semi-private space to essentially hide in. The mostly familiar faces of Bryan and Mac's friends also helped with my anxiety, plus a lot of liquid courage. Although he engaged with everyone, Bryan stayed close to me, being a constant presence that helped keep me relatively calm. My pulse pounded, and I was hyperaware of my busy surroundings—including Bryan's knee resting against mine, and how I wanted more contact from him. Leaning my weight on his shoulder and watching *A New Hope* sounded like a wonderful way to spend the night, but we could do that any time. Mac only turned—um... I actually had no idea how old Mac was. Likely thirty or thirty-one.

One bass-heavy song morphed into another, and everyone in our booth got keyed up. Mac and Blake shot up first, leading the way to the dance floor. Only Bryan and I remained seated.

"You don't want to go with them?" I spoke directly into his ear to be heard over the music.

"I want to keep you company."

"Go dance. I'll still be here when you guys get back." Bryan cast concerned eyes over me then nodded and followed after his friends.

If I thought Bryan looked good playing baseball, he looked like a god dancing. Dancing in public for fun as a concept never made sense to me until I laid eyes on Bryan and his friends. Everyone smiled and moved to the music—sometimes alone, sometimes with each other, and sometimes with strangers. Maxim stood off on the periphery watching, all stoic and serious, but everyone else looked like they were having the best time. As I watched them, nothing else seemed to exist, and I wondered if that was how they felt while engaging in the act.

Everyone, to me, looked like they were good dancers, though my eyes kept tracking back to Bryan. He had his hands on Blake's hips and was between her and a guy I didn't recognize—a stranger.

The newcomer stepped in closer—and grabbed Bryan's ass. Bryan spun around, and the new guy worked himself flush against Bryan, grinding and writhing to the music. Irrational anger surged through me, and I saw red. I moved to stand, but Bryan stepped back from the cling-on, smiled, and said something in his ear, then resumed dancing with Blake and Axel.

I leaned back against the booth, though relaxation didn't come. I was glad he didn't go for that guy's advances, but I was still angry that that guy thought he had the right to touch Bryan like that. Not wanting to think about it any longer, I poured myself a new drink, forgoing the mix, and tossed it back in one gulp. Rinse and repeat.

When I finished pouring my third drink, Maxim returned to the booth and nodded to me as he sat down and nursed his own cocktail. I enjoyed that he was a man of few words, but his silence could be intense. I didn't mind it that night. I didn't mind much of anything after the tequila hit me with the force of a charging bull.

The bench next to me dipped, and I turned to see Bryan, skin moistened with sweat. "Hey," he said.

I held my glass up between us before I leaned in and replied, "I'm a little drunk. Maybe a lot."

He smirked and pulled my hand with the glass up toward his nose then reached for the tequila bottle and added a generous shot to both of our glasses. I missed the warmth and contact when his hand left mine, but new warmth spread through me when I tossed back the clear alcohol.

"You good?" Mac asked, suddenly next to me.

I gave him a thumbs-up and a punchy smile, then he told me about the real-life Jean Grey he found by the bar, and I had to laugh.

"You certainly do have a type," I said to him.

With a drink in hand, gesturing away, he said, "I am a man of many vices and redheaded women are at the top of that list."

"You're going to have the whitest kids ever someday, *rubito,*" Axel quipped, eliciting laughter from anyone close enough to hear the remark. Maxim even cracked a smile.

The night pulsed on and the group ventured out to the dance floor again and had returned when I finished my sixth drink—or maybe it was the seventh, I wasn't really keeping score. Bryan checked in on me again while everyone else did shots. Once more, they left to go dance, but Mac grabbed my wrist and hauled me along with him, insisting that I *had* to dance for at least one song.

My tongue felt heavy and didn't work when I tried to voice my protestations. Surrounded by a swarm of moving people with my head a mess, I began to panic. I pulled back, overestimating the force the act required and tripped backward, bumping into a solid body. An apology tried to form on my tongue when I looked up into Bryan's sage-green eyes. I felt his hot grip on my arms more than I saw him move to touch me and craved more of his heat. He pulled me against his chest and my hands instinctively clung to his waist.

My eyes darted around to the people around us, and despite the fact that no one looked our way, I felt like they were all going to bury me. I tightened my grip on Bryan and shivered when his stubble brushed against my neck.

"You're okay, Elijah. Just close your eyes and focus on me and the music," he said.

My eyes fluttered closed and I gave all of my trust to him. One of his arms wrapped around my waist, holding me firm and close, while the other found purchase at my nape. Bryan's fingers curled into my hair as he swayed us, slow and tentative at first, leisurely picking up the pace as my body melted against his.

By the second song we moved as one; I couldn't tell where I ended and he began, and it was intoxicating. The whole place smelled like alcohol and sweat, yet I thought I could smell Bryan's sweetness when I nuzzled the junction of his neck and collarbone. I noticed how sweet he smelled after we started getting closer, whether it was through hugs or sitting next to him on the couch. I'd seen his body wash and it wasn't from that. It was probably silly and all in my head, but he smelled like vanilla and lemons to me most of the time—even fresh out of the shower.

With my face buried in his neck, I drowned in the scent —his scent. It seemed so much stronger that night than it ever had before, and I found myself wanting more.

Does he taste as good as he smells?

The thought was gone just as quickly as it had passed through my mind, but its echoes were louder than the relentless music. I lifted my head enough to brush my cheek against Bryan's, relishing in the scrape from his beard. We were so close that our noses brushed, and I could feel his breath on my lips. My eyes were still closed, causing me to jump in surprise when he rubbed his cheek against mine, almost like he was nuzzling. No. It was exactly like that.

I chanced opening my eyes and saw a look from Bryan I hadn't seen before. It was almost pained. His forehead was creased and his mouth tight, and his eyes burned. He looked like a man waging a war within himself, but I wasn't sure what that war was. He bit his bottom lip and flexed his hand on my lower back, and I thought he was going to kiss me. No one had ever looked at me the way he was, but I somehow knew what the look meant.

I felt lightheaded, and it had nothing to do with the alcohol. Bryan's tongue raked across his lips, and I groaned inadvertently, hoping the music drowned it out. He leaned back in, brushing our noses once more, and I held my breath. Time stood still while I ceased to exist, paralyzed in his arms. Then he squeezed my nape and sighed in a way that told me one side had prevailed in his war. He shook his head—more to himself than for me it seemed—and took a small step back from me.

Even with his hands still on me, I felt his absence, and my stomach twisted; I felt like I was going to be sick. I abruptly excused myself and headed straight for the bathrooms. There was a line, but luckily it wasn't long and within a couple of minutes I stood at a sink and splashed cold water on my face. I hadn't noticed while we were dancing, but I was rock hard.

I white-knuckled the edge of the sink and sank my head between my shoulders. It was too much. Everything was just too much, and I needed to go home. How long had I been this turned on? Oh God, what if Bryan noticed? And why? Why was I—

I lifted my head, and all thoughts abruptly stopped when I met Bryan's gaze in the mirror. He was leaning against the wall, working his jaw like he might have been contemplating speaking or grinding his teeth. I took a deep breath and turned around to face him, but he didn't come to me. He dropped his eyes from mine and seemed unusually stiff and jerky, like he didn't know what to do with himself. I recognized it immediately because it was my daily reality. I closed the distance between us and reached for him, faltering before

I reached him. Determined to overcome whatever the hell was happening to me, I grabbed his arm and watched his shoulders relax.

"I… I think I'm going to go home," I said, not having to speak as loudly as before.

Bryan lifted his head and replied with, "I'll take you. You've had a lot to drink."

I wanted to tell him to stay and have fun with his friends; however, I just nodded and let him lead me out. He texted someone from the cab, but my eyes closed, and I drifted off before I could inquire.

I woke up sweaty and in my bed with Prince curled up by my feet. My head was pounding harder than the music from the club and my mouth tasted of bile. I moved to check the time on my bedside alarm clock and froze when I noticed my arm was bare. I was wearing a T-shirt I hadn't had on last night.

Ugh. Last night—rather, five hours ago based on the time. I couldn't remember getting home. I recall getting in a cab with Bryan after we… fuck. The events of the night flooded back all at once. I thought Bryan was going to kiss me, and I thought I *wanted* him to. The way he smelled and felt against me, so warm and comforting, stirred my dick to life again.

I squeezed my balls and whimpered at how overly sensitive I was. I was transported back to dancing with Bryan and couldn't think about anything other than how good he'd felt against me—how *right* he felt.

"No, no, no." I stood and dug through the discarded baseball costume on the floor in search of my phone. A flashing red light in my periphery caught my attention, and I found my phone on the damn nightstand next to the clock. I unlocked it and saw a few unread texts from Bryan from when he must have dropped me off.

B: I took Prince out for a walk when we got in. You threw up when I was gone, which is why I changed your shirt

B: I didn't want to leave your door unlocked, but I thought I should go home, so I have your key. I can bring it by tomorrow for you

B: We can talk then

That's it? I wanted to reply, but I didn't know what to say. Thank you would have been a good start, but beyond that I was lost. I had one other person who could help me, and my fingers flew as I typed out a message to her. It was before seven in the morning, so I wasn't expecting an immediate reply. I locked my phone, got a glass of water and some Advil, and got back in bed.

"I don't know what to do," I said to Eve and Samir. I sat next to her on their couch, while Samir was in an adjacent chair. He'd offered to give us privacy when I arrived, but I wanted all the help I could possibly get. I'd already given them a quick rundown of the night's events, although I left out the more embarrassing details. "That's weird, right? I was really drunk and confused."

"Oh, pet. It's not weird. Alcohol and close proximity are a dangerous combination for anyone," Eve offered.

"For a minute I even thought he was going to k-kiss me… and I… did nothing to stop him. He didn't kiss me, though." I smiled bitterly and rubbed my palms together between my knees. "He pulled away, and I don't know if I'm relieved or disappointed over it. I feel like I don't know anything anymore. What if I was just drunk and imagined it all?"

"Eli, if Bryan *did* want to kiss you, how do you feel about that now?" Samir asked evenly.

"I... I don't know."

Eve placed her hand over mine and gently squeezed. "Think about it—really think."

I was confused about a lot, mainly why I was feeling what I was, and where the feelings came from, but I knew the answer to the question Eve and Samir asked. "I... wanted him to kiss me. I think I still do. I don't know why, but the idea"—I looked between them, feeling embarrassed—"excites me—in ways I'm not used to."

"Eli—"

"I don't understand what's happening to me," I scraped out, barely above a whisper. "What if he knows now and things are weird between us? Oh God, what if he doesn't want to see me anymore?" My panic spiked, making my skin break out in sweat when my phone buzzed in my pocket. I pulled it out to see a text from Bryan, right on cue. "It's him."

"What does it say?" Eve asked.

"He's checking to see how I'm feeling and if I want him to bring anything particular to eat." Normal. He seemed normal, but you couldn't ever really tell with a text.

"I don't think you have to worry about him not wantin' ya. The best thing you can do is talk to him."

She was probably right. But we all knew I was shit at talking, especially if it meant things with Bryan could change.

When I saw Bryan, I'd chickened out, and carried on as if last night hadn't happened. Bryan brought over a double pepperoni pizza with green peppers on half, just how I liked it. He didn't mention last night either and was unusually reserved and distant until we sat down to watch *Point Break*.

He sat down first at the end of the couch where he always did, and I sat down next to him before I thought about whether I should.

Second-guessing my every move sounded exhausting and it was exactly what I didn't want, so I just kept my mouth shut and carried on as I normally would; I finished my pizza and leaned on his shoulder while we watched the movie— with Prince alternating between lying at our feet and in his lap.

Things were completely normal with Bryan in the weeks following what I dubbed "the incident." Kind of. He dropped the guarded act and behaved normally with me, though I wasn't quite the same. I didn't outwardly act any different, but I was more *aware* of Bryan, and specifically, how much my eyes followed him. The fucking inopportune boners kept springing up as well, making me feel like a hormonal teenager in every respect.

Eve suggested I try to talk to Bryan about what was going on, and if I couldn't, to try to process and sort it out for myself at the very least. I tried to—I really did—but I only came up with more questions. I was clearly attracted to Bryan. The erection I hid while watching him play baseball made it so I couldn't try to deny that. But I wasn't gay. I'd never felt an attraction to another man before in my life, and my one encounter all those years ago went a long way in solidifying that fact. Then I started getting aroused from seeing and even thinking about *him*.

I had the joy of seeing Mac stark naked, wandering out of his room in search of breakfast, last week, and it did nothing for me. Yet when I pictured Bryan in such a state, I had to lock myself in the bathroom and will my traitorous dick to behave. It hadn't even been that bad when I was a teen.

An upside to the situation was that I found inspiration in Bryan. I dreamed about him in vivid colors and shapes and wanted to recreate the images if I could. I purchased four small canvases and spent my solitary evenings painting.

My thoughts were a fucked-up mess, but everything I felt looked so clear in brushstrokes.

FOURTEEN

BRYAN

THE NEXT FEW WEEKS FLEW BY as if all time were stuck in light speed—the past few months in general had. Summer was long gone, and the first snow was expected any day. The three-month anniversary for Eat Cake was two short weeks away, and I was informed by Mac that it was a huge deal and that we needed to "turn up." I was indeed proud of myself and the business, but Mac truly did love any excuse to party, and that was fine by me.

I was closing up after a busy Friday, trying to find some calm in the familiar task of cleaning my workspace. Between exceedingly early mornings, long days, shuffling my hobbies and commitments, and more trips to the bank than I'd had in my entire life—I was in need of some chill time.

Then there was Eli.

I'd almost ruined things on Halloween. Blaming the alcohol and the atmosphere would have been easy, but I wasn't all that drunk, and I knew it was wrong. My resolve nearly shattered that night, and I worried that I'd shown him my hand and he wouldn't like what he saw. I was so drunk with lust that I almost convinced myself that he wanted me in return. The poor guy was wasted, and I nearly kissed him —it was a fucking disaster.

By some stroke of good fortune, he either didn't remember what happened or he interpreted it for something other than what it was. I had every intention of apologizing and begging for forgiveness, but the subject was never broached. Eli treated me as if everything was status quo and showed no signs of pulling away from me. If anything, we'd slowly grown closer.

This was the first Friday night in over a month that I wouldn't be spending with him, either at my place or his. I missed him already at just the thought of not seeing him, but I was looking forward to a quiet evening alone. Friday night meant Mac would be out as well—he only really stayed in when Eli and I were over.

The sound of the door opening out front made me utter a curse at myself for having forgotten to lock up after closing again. I dried my hands on my pants and headed out front, already apologizing and explaining that we were closed. The words stalled when I saw Mac there, holding a duffel.

"Pack up; we're going to the gym tonight."

"Dude, I'm tired," I whined. I still kept up with my workouts, but I'd been slacking off this week and declining all of Mac's invites.

"Nuh-uh. That wasn't a request. I brought you a change of clothes."

There was no use putting up a fight once Mac made up his mind about something, so I agreed and finished cleaning before we set off.

My muscles ached in all the right ways as I lowered myself into the hot tub next to Mac. We'd worked with free weights and hit the rowers for some cardio, so I was ready to pass out after being lazy for a week. While working with the weights he'd asked me how the business was going. I gave him a quick rundown, essentially saying things were going better than expected, and that I was going to look into hiring two more people and opening on Sundays as well. Eli had mentioned that starting with Sunday would be a good idea. I pitched a few menu ideas to Mac, but he was noncommittal and demanded a taste test for breakfast.

"I miss you," I said to him after we both settled.

Before the launch I'd been working part time while formulating my business plan and saw Mac for the majority of the day. Now that I had the bakery, I was usually up by five thirty and there by six to make everything fresh for our eight o'clock opening. Mac usually hibernated until ten or eleven unless he had a Skype meeting or needed to be present at the office for when the shit hit the fan. Not being around to make him breakfast and just hang out sucked.

Then my time was divided even more between him and Eli, though the situation improved when Eli started coming over to our place. I loved spending time with them together and was thrilled that they got on so well.

"I know, man. But isn't this what growing up is like? You had to leave the nest sometime," he teased.

I snorted and splashed him like a mature adult. "Maybe I don't wanna grow up."

"Nah. Being a Lost Boy wouldn't suit you—and we both know I'd be Peter Pan, so that's out. Growing up isn't your problem, but Eli sure as fuck is."

"Ouch. Straight to the point, huh?"

"It's like that," he said with a sympathetic smile.

"Did you see us? On your birthday, I mean."

Mac's laugh echoed in the empty room. "Bry, everyone saw. Half of the damn club wanted in on that action."

I groaned and slid deeper into the water. "I fucked up and got carried away."

"I don't know; it looked pretty fucking mutual to me."

"As much as he thinks he's this prickly outsider, Eli thrives on contact. He's very tactile when we're alone, though never in a sexual way. He was drunk and in an unfamiliar place; it's no surprise that he held on to me."

Mac sighed in frustration, sinking down with me. "You're both hopelessly clueless—and not in a cute, endearing kind of way anymore. Now that shit is bordering on tragic. Okay, that's a *little* hyperbolic, but damn, Bry."

"What do you want me to do? We've been over this. I can't have him—and I won't give him up, so don't even suggest it," I snapped.

"Easy. Now that I've met him, I'd never suggest you give up. Quite the contrary actually. I'm frustrated that you're so content to pine away and not fight for him." Mac said it like it was the easiest thing in the world. He had a tendency to see things in black and white—in a fun versus boring kind of way.

"Content? This isn't what I wanted, but what other choice do I have? I—" I sighed and took a deep breath to calm down. Getting angry with Mac when he was only trying to help was a dick move, and I needed to stop. "I love him, Mac. I really fucking love him." Saying it out loud was the last step in making it real. I'd known for months that I loved him—now it was *real*, and I felt even more fucked than before. I tried to say more, but my voice broke and my lips trembled with the effort.

Mac scooted closer and stroked the back of my hair before letting his arm drop around my shoulder. We had always been pretty touchy-feely, but this was new, intimate territory for us. He was comforting me, and I needed it.

"I know you do. Admitting it is the first step."

I snorted and dropped my head, worried that I might cry if I kept looking at him.

"I mean it, you dick. I'm proud of you, even if you do drive me crazy. You'll figure out the rest."

The rest? I just sighed and leaned into his touch, wondering what Eli was up to.

IN BED THAT NIGHT, I couldn't relax. I missed Eli too damn much, and Mac's cryptic words left me feeling unsettled. I reached for my phone to check the time and saw that it was just after midnight—too late to call Eli. What would I have said anyway? Nothing that couldn't wait until a reasonable hour, so I wouldn't look like a psycho stalker.

I gave it half an hour before I caved and texted him. YouTube and porn failed to distract me, and I texted him like the pathetic mess of a man I was, half worked up thanks to the latter. I wasn't expecting a reply and jumped when one came through right away.

E: Yes, I'm awake
B: What're you up to?

Ugh. I might as well have asked him what he was wearing and been done with it.

E: I just got out of the shower and am in bed now
E: What about you? Prince and I missed seeing you tonight

He missed me too? I had no hope of falling asleep after reading that. Forget about the fact that he was fresh from the shower and smelling like the ocean and *maybe* naked.

Jesus Christ.

B: I'm in bed too. Utterly drained. I missed you guys tonight too.

B: If you're free tomorrow, wanna grab some lunch? There's a new Vietnamese place that opened up a couple blocks from my place

E: No

No? Aww, shit. My stomach churned, and my panic went from zero to one hundred in half a second. Was it rational? Absolutely not. Did it matter at the time? Nope. My fingers were typing out a frantic reply asking what I did wrong and apologizing when a new message came through.

E: Ugh. Sorry. Prince bumped me and the message sent before I finished typing

E: No to trying the new place tomorrow. I'd much rather have your cooking, if you don't mind

Relief washed over me, though it didn't quite quell the burn in my cheeks from having overreacted so quickly. I wasn't the kind of person who jumped to sweeping conclusions like that, but Eli had me all fucked up in every way.

B: OK. What do you want me to make?

E: Will you laugh at me if I say spaghetti?

B: I won't lie. I am smiling, but I'd never laugh at you

B: Oh! There was something else. Mac wanted to go out and celebrate the bakery's three month anni

B: IDK if that's a real thing or not, but it's an excuse to celebrate so I won't take that away from him. Wanna come?

E: Would you be mad if I take a pass this time?

B: Of course not

E: I do want to celebrate with you, though. I just don't think I'm up for another two-day hangover

B: Hahaha, that's understandable

E: I'll make it up to you. You can pick whatever you want and I'll do it. I promise

Whatever I wanted? Nope—not going to let my mind run away with that one.

B: Deal. You'll regret those words

FIFTEEN

ELI

W HEN I PROMISED BRYAN I'D do anything, I didn't really know what to expect. I meant it, but it just kind of came out in the spur of the moment. I couldn't see his face, and I hadn't wanted him to be sad or upset with me.

What I didn't expect was to find myself sitting in the middle of a packed karaoke bar on a Saturday night. A couple had just finished a duet of "Ring of Fire" and were met with applause before the chatter of all of the tables filled the room with what was almost a buzz. I sat next to Bryan at a small round table for two—it was the only way to hear him and it helped aid me in not freaking the fuck out.

We shared pitchers of beer and various finger-food appetizers while enjoying the ever-amusing amateur singers. Some people were skilled enough to be professionals while some were rather terrible but had a good time. I had a lot of respect for anyone brave enough to walk up there in front of a bar full of strangers, let alone do that *and* sing.

Bryan offered me the last mozzarella stick, which I broke in half for us to share. I popped it in my mouth and used a napkin to wipe my fingers clean of crumbs and grease. Bryan had done the same and finished his glass of beer. He raised his brows, and gave me a roguish grin.

"Wanna try it with me?" he asked.

"Uh… try what?"

He nodded his head toward the small stage, smile growing wider when my eyes went wide. "Fuck no. Are you crazy? I could never—"

Bryan's laughter cut off my tirade. He wasn't just laughing, no; it was that side-clenching laughing that couldn't be contained. I crossed my arms and waited him out, hoping I wore my best unimpressed pout.

"I'm glad you're so amused. I thought you said you'd never laugh at me?"

He took a couple of deep breaths to calm himself and raised a brow at me critically. "Oh, come on. This doesn't count. You just caught me off guard with how adamantly you were against it. I figured you'd say no, but not quite with such enthusiasm."

"I can't think of anything worse at the moment," I mumbled.

"Would you be terribly opposed to me doing a song?"

Huh? "*You* sing?" I must have sounded far more skeptical than I thought because he snorted and laughed again.

Bryan shrugged noncommittally. "Would you like to find out?"

I nodded, and he went up to choose a song. He smiled from ear to ear when he found his pick and stepped up on the small stage. The few seconds of silence before the song played were long enough for me to realize that I didn't need to be up there to feel like the room was going to collapse in on me. Bryan looked unaffected, but my secondhand anxiety ran wild until he sang the first note of a song that started without any backing music. Oh, it was a song I knew—and everyone else in the place based on the happy cheers.

The opening notes of Queen's "Fat Bottomed Girls" had most of the bar singing along as Bryan strutted around the stage like he'd been there his whole life. Seeing him thrive and be cheered on quelled my anxiety, and I watched in wonder as he gave a part of himself up for the room that I hadn't seen before. He oozed charisma and sex appeal—he always did, but this was another level.

When he locked eyes with me, I felt a wave of something warm sweep through my body again. Adoration, perhaps? I certainly did adore him. He made me feel like I was the only person in the room, like I had all of his focus and he was singing just to please me. The thought made me indescribably happy.

The song came to an end, and everyone cheered and clapped for him. A rowdy table of women near the stage shouted for more and a few others followed suit. Bryan looked to me with a lip-biting half smile, almost like he was seeking my permission. No—that's exactly what he was doing.

I nodded at him, and he picked another crowd-pleasing favorite: "Another One Bites the Dust." He sang five songs in total—all Queen—and continued to look my way, making me feel like no one else existed.

We took Prince out for a run when we got back to my place. And by run I meant drunken sprint. Bryan took her off-leash and let her chase him around on the empty grass in front of my apartment building. He was so uncoordinated and clumsy; watching her pull on his pant legs and trip him up had me in tears. He protested helplessly as she assaulted his face with sloppy kisses, tail wagging nonstop. Seeing Bryan being so silly with Prince always brought me joy. He fit so perfectly into every part of my life—not that there were many facets, but that wasn't the point.

I'd thought I was content before, but Bryan was so very clearly the missing component in my existence. I couldn't picture being without him, whether he was being silly with my dog or comforting me when I was on the brink of losing my shit. Fuck, just sitting beside him felt good. I felt his absence when he was gone. Painting worked as a nice distraction, though it didn't remotely replace him. When he texted me late last Friday night I couldn't stop smiling. I knew it was silly, but just knowing he was thinking about me as well had settled me for the night.

"Eli, help! She's relentless," he cried, half laughing.

I walked over to the mess of them on the ground and called Prince over. She came immediately and sat at my feet, allowing Bryan to stand and wipe his face on his sweater. We looked at each other for a few moments and burst out laughing. I nearly tripped myself and fell over, but Bryan managed to close the distance between us and steady me. The cool air disappeared when he touched me, replaced by his immeasurable heat.

We went upstairs and collapsed on the couch after I refreshed Prince's water and Bryan washed his face.

"Puppy kisses are great, but they are fuckin' messy," he said.

"You might be her new favorite. She's crazy for you."

Bryan sank into the couch with his arms resting along the back. "Nah. You're still her favorite. She listens to you. I think she thinks I'm one of her toys, to be honest. That's okay, though." He let his head drop back onto the cushion. "I don't mind."

The couch felt so good after the excitement from downstairs, but I wanted more; I wanted to be closer. I leaned on Bryan like I normally would, though his arm was up, so I ended up on his chest. I wondered if he'd say something, comment on how strange he thought it was. He didn't. I settled against his chest, breathing in his sweet vanilla and citrus scent, while a flash of familiarity crept up on me. We hadn't done this before, but I felt almost nostalgic, as if we had.

"I can't believe you like Queen."

"Correction: I *love* Queen. They're my favorite band." I couldn't see it, but I heard the smile in his voice.

"I didn't know you could sing either." Bryan's singing voice was higher than his speaking one. He was well suited to Queen's music, and I honestly could have listened to him sing all night.

"I love to sing. I forgot how much so. I used to sing Mac's little sister to sleep when we'd visit his family. And… no. Never mind."

I craned my neck up and got an eyeful of his scruffy chin. "What? You can't just stop like that."

"Fair enough." Bryan sighed and giggled to himself. "I used to sing to my horse. And the calves. I swear, it calmed them before they went to sleep."

The thought of him singing to his animals brought a smile to my face. He truly was the best. "My mom used to do that for me. God, I'd forgotten all about that. She sang 'Sweet Child O' Mine' and this one Al Green song a lot. Something about a broken heart. I don't remember, it's been so long."

Bryan was quiet a moment then began humming a song I instantly recognized as the one I'd forgotten the name to. "That one?" he asked. I nodded against his chest. "It's a great one. 'How Can You Mend a Broken Heart.'"

Fragments of memories of my mom played before my eyes. Her stroking my hair behind my ear when I was sad, her holding me while I cried after being made fun of at school, her singing me to sleep.

"I can sing for you sometime... if you want," Bryan offered. "I really don't mind."

I snorted and smirked. "Where have you been my entire life?"

"I waited for you, you know," he said, after a few beats of silence.

"Hmm? What?"

"After the shoot. We'd agreed to go out after, so I could meet your dog. You were so cute, and I was so eager to see you again outside of work. So I waited for you. In the parking lot with my keys in my hand. When some of the other performers came out, I asked if they'd seen you and a girl said she saw you heading toward the back exit in a hurry."

"I'm really sorry about that, Bryan. I—"

"S'okay. Really. I'm just glad you ended up being okay. I worried about what might have happened to you; if maybe you got a call about your dog and you had to jet. Occasionally I wondered about you. Over the years, I mean. I only had your first name, so I couldn't find you. So I just wondered. I imagined what you might be doing and hoped that you and your dog were happy. Isn't that strange?" Bryan laughed to himself, but there was no humor in it. "Then I saw you again after all these years, and it felt like it was a sign —sort of a second chance for me that I missed out on back then. Shit, I should stop rambling. In fact, I'm going to go home." He stood, careful not to jar me too much, then headed straight for the door.

"Why are you leaving?" I got up and went after him. He already had his boots on when I reached him. "What's wrong?"

"I just—I need to go home right now. It's late, and I'm drunk and saying stupid shit. It's better if I leave now. I'll text you tomorrow." He opened the door and left without a backward glance.

I stood there completely still, trying to figure out where the hell things went wrong. Why would he react like that? He looked almost scared before he left.

I should go after him. And say what? I didn't understand what had upset him, and I didn't want to make things worse. I paced the open space in my entryway, going over what Bryan had said to me. I remembered that we made plans to hang out, but I was such a mess after the shoot that I couldn't stand the thought of him, or anyone else who knew what I'd done, seeing me. I'd fled to my car down the street, cash in my pocket, and cried, full of shame and self-loathing.

I hadn't spared a thought for Rhett Ryder and the idea that he might be waiting to see me. But he had. He'd thought about me, too. Why would he? *Second chance.* I looked at Prince, who'd followed us to the door.

"What did he mean by that? A second chance for what?" Why did he have so much fear in his eyes when he left? It was a look I recognized because it was what I felt when I looked at him. Fear of change, fear of rejection. Why would he fear that? Unless—

No, he couldn't. *But what if he did?* A hundred different emotions and urges pulled me in all directions, yet one pull was stronger than the others. I opened the door and ran out into the hall, only to skid to a stop when I saw Bryan standing with his forehead resting against the wall outside of my apartment.

He lifted his head at the ruckus I made, but before he could get a word out, I stepped into his space, closed my eyes, and pressed my trembling lips to his. My uncertainty melted away once I felt his lips on mine and everything felt *right.* When he put his hands on my waist and kissed me back, I felt *whole*. He'd been what was missing this whole time, and I was too stupid to notice it.

His tongue swept into my mouth and skimmed the roof of my mouth, making me moan. He growled into my mouth and tightened his grip in response, and my dick took notice. I pulled back before I embarrassed myself by doing something stupid like jizzing in my fucking pants. Taking a deep breath, I took another step back from Bryan until I was out of his grasp. I breathed in and out a couple of times to reorient myself, blinking the stupor out of my eyes.

"Why?" Bryan asked. His forehead creased with confusion. I wanted to kiss him again and erase that look from his face.

I looked around the empty hallway and asked if he'd come back inside. Once we had some privacy, the weight of what I'd just done hit me and a flush crept up my chest and neck.

"Eli—"

"No. I should probably talk first." *Since I* did *just throw myself at you.* "Um. So, I kissed you." I dropped my eyes and focused on Prince dancing around Bryan's feet, trying to get his attention. He gave in and reached down to pet her.

"Maybe we should go sit down and talk about this?"

I nodded and mechanically marched over to the couch, plunking down in the middle. Bryan took his usual spot. "I kissed you. And I was going to apologize for not asking, but it just dawned on me that you kissed me back. Like, a lot."

Bryan smiled nervously. "I did."

"So, you're not mad?" I needed to hear it. At that point it was pretty obvious, but I needed him to say it.

"I'm not remotely mad, Eli. I'm happy, though I'm a little confused."

I huffed out a laugh. "Believe me, I am too. I'm just so relieved you're not angry with me."

"I'm so fucking far from angry—you have no idea."

"I hope you'll tell me when I'm done talking. To put it frankly, I think I'm in love with you." Bryan's eyes were saucers, and he just stared at me, unblinking. "Should I not have said that?"

"No, you just surprised me. I don't know why, I wouldn't have expected that kind of confession to come any other way from you. Then again, I never thought I'd hear those words from you. Are you sure?"

"I'm pretty damn sure. I've never been in love before, but if it means thinking about someone for nearly every waking hour, wanting to see them... wanting to touch them, then it's safe to say that I do. Love you, I mean. I thought it was admiration, and perhaps it was in the beginning. You were this new, exciting person who somehow gave a shit about me. I don't know when exactly those feelings changed, but they did. And now I can't stop thinking about you." I licked my dry lips and swallowed to try and wet my throat. "I wondered what you might taste like, and now I'm glad I know.

"You're my best friend, Bryan. You've given me so much and helped me grow more than I ever thought was possible. We've done so much together, but now I want more. I want *you*. These feelings confused me when they first started, but I'm not confused anymore. I understand that this is probably a lot to just lay on you, and I'm sorry about that. I felt like I needed to say it."

"I don't fucking believe this," Bryan said, almost breathlessly. "I've wanted you since the day we met. Since the very first damn day. I've been in love with you for months. I—" He stopped himself and balled his fist on his thigh. "Is this really happening?"

I picked up Bryan's hand and laced his fingers with mine, reveling in how good such a simple act felt. "I can assure you that this is really happening. Do you mind if I kiss you again?" He shook his head, so I kissed his fingertips, paying close attention to each one as thanks for all the comfort they'd brought me.

Bryan sucked in a sharp breath. He leaned toward me, brushing his nose against mine, just like he had while we were dancing. His scruff scraped my jaw, and I moaned, eliciting a throaty laugh from him. "You remember this, don't you?"

"Yes," I replied. Well, it was more like a strangled whimper.

He continued brushing our cheeks and noses, ghosting his lips over mine with each pass. "I wanted to kiss you so badly that night."

"So kiss me now."

The kiss started slow and exploratory—all lips and soft caresses. He kissed each corner of my mouth and a spot on my jaw before joining our lips. His left hand cupped the back of my head while he pulled me closer with his right until I was practically in his lap. I liked the way it felt to be held by him, and my body reacted, just like out in the hall. When his tongue drew across the roof of my mouth again, I moaned—even louder than before. I forgot to breathe and pulled away gasping and dazed and needing more.

Bryan took one look at me and pushed forward, pinning me flat on my back with the weight of his body. He claimed my mouth again at the same time he ground his hips into mine, and I knew without a doubt that he was just as turned on as I was.

The feeling of him grinding against me was incredible. It was unlike anything I'd experienced with anyone before. Every cell in my body reacted to Bryan; his voice, his scent, his all-encompassing touch. He kissed me deeper and harder with ragged breaths while his grip on me tightened. I was gasping, and on the verge of coming when he abruptly leaned up and blinked down at me with wide eyes. His lips were rosier than usual.

"I'm sorry. I'm getting carried away. I didn't mean to attack you like that." His chest heaved with exertion, and his dick was hard against my hip.

"You can keep doing that."

Bryan dropped his head against my shoulder and groaned. "I don't think I have the self-control to continue just kissing you right now." He lifted his head and his cheeks were flushed, whether it was with lust or embarrassment, I couldn't tell. Maybe it was both.

"Oh," I said. Based on the way he'd been grinding against me and his words, I figured he meant sex. I wanted that with him at some point, but it might have been a bit much that night.

He snorted a laugh and lifted his hips from mine with a low growl. "Yes, 'oh.' We don't have to rush this. And we should talk about it some more after we get some rest." He leaned up off of me completely and extended a hand to help me up.

Once I was righted and thinking more clearly, slowing things down did sound like a smart idea. It wasn't the one my dick wanted at that moment, but I knew Bryan had a point. I'd gone so long not wanting sex, and abstaining another night—or however many nights Bryan felt were necessary—wouldn't kill me. I mean, probably not. "I guess you're right. Will you, um… will you stay with me?"

Bryan leaned over and kissed me chastely in a soft kiss. He smiled at me and told me he would love to stay, and that was all I needed to hear to forget about my newfound lust.

We took turns getting ready for bed. I gave Bryan my extra toothbrush from the multipack I bought and waited in bed for him with Prince curled up at my feet and the lamp on. I didn't know if I should've kept my clothes on or taken them off, but keeping them on seemed like the safer, less presumptuous choice.

Bryan entered the room wearing his boxers and a T-shirt he must have had on under his sweater. "I'd offer you a fresh shirt, but I don't think any of mine would fit you. You can just take it off if you want."

He cocked an eyebrow at me and one corner of his mouth twitched into a smirk. He grabbed the hem of his shirt and pulled it over his head in a single motion. The light from the lamp cast over the dips and ridges of his abdominal muscles and the hair centered near the middle of his pecs. I wasn't an authority on men's bodies by any means, but his seemed ideal to me. Not too bulky, yet strong without looking like a roided-out mess.

My eyes traveled down to his belly button and the trail of dark hair leading down, under the waistband of his black boxer briefs. I bit my bottom lip at the sight of the bulge in his trunks, suddenly imagining what he might look like completely naked.

"If you keep looking at me like that it's going to be very difficult to keep my hands off you tonight," he drawled.

"Would that be so bad?"

"Be good, please. Today was a lot for both of us," he pleaded.

"You better hurry up and get under the blankets then."

He walked around the bed and slid in behind me, snug against my back with an arm draped over my waist. His warmth and sweet smell made the idea of going to sleep much more inviting if it meant being in his arms all night.

Prince came up to investigate and kiss Bryan's arm before returning to the foot of the bed. We bid each other good-night and I shut the light off, faltering in the action when

Bryan's lips pressed against the back of my neck. He nuzzled into my nape and whispered that he loved me, which was how we ended up lazily making out in bed until we fell asleep. I wasn't sure who dozed first, but it didn't really matter.

SIXTEEN

BRYAN

I woke up with the ocean in my nose and the heat of the sun against my body. I opened one eye to reveal a mess of short brown hair and smiled to myself, relieved that last night hadn't been some sort of illusion or cruel dream. Eli had kissed me *and* told me he loved me. The joy and happiness I felt down to every fiber of my being was immeasurable. I even felt fucking tingly—in one place more so than the rest of my body.

I tried to move my foot, but it didn't budge. I lifted my head to see what was going on and smiled when I caught sight of Prince soundly sleeping with her head resting on my ankle. Even in sleep, she looked like she was smiling. The urge to reach down and gently squeeze her cheeks was strong, though I had other urges that far outweighed that one.

Morning wood was a fact of life and nothing outside of the ordinary for me. It was different today because I was in bed with Eli and my dick was firmly pressed against the crack of his ass. If I stayed wedged up against him there was no hope of it simply going away like it did other mornings. Very slowly, I tried to inch back without rousing him from sleep.

I failed.

"Where are you going?" he asked, his voice thick with sleep. He sounded gruff and way too sexy, which only made me grow harder.

"Nowhere. I'm still right here."

He hummed his approval and shifted back against me, making me bite my tongue to keep from moaning at the friction. He moved again and chuckled softly. "Are you turned on right now?"

So fucking blunt—just one of the things I loved about this man. I bit back my smile and kissed his nape. "Yes, I am. I tried not to wake you."

Eli turned around in my arms and looked up at me with half-lidded eyes. "You don't have to move away. I was hoping you'd want to stay."

"Of course I do." I pulled him close and kissed him, first on his nose, then on his lips. "I'm not leaving. I just didn't want you to wake up... ah, like you did, and think I wanted to... okay, it's dumb saying it out loud."

"Is that why you never told me how you felt?"

"Yeah. I didn't want you to think I expected more than just your friendship. You trusted me, and I didn't want to betray that or pressure you into doing what I wanted." I couldn't live with myself had I let either of those things happen.

"You're too good for me. I've thought that since day one, but now I know it to be true more than ever. I don't know why you love me, though I'm so thankful that you do."

I was going to kiss him again, but he took the initiative and closed the short distance between our lips. I managed to free my trapped leg and slung it over Eli to pull him closer. His hips met mine, and I faltered in the kiss when I felt his rock-hard cock against mine.

I flipped him onto his back and was over him in seconds.

Morning breath be damned, there wasn't anything that was going to keep me from him. He stared up at me, panting with parted lips and dilating pupils. I fisted the back of his hair and tugged his head back, exposing his neck and all of those little dots I'd longed to connect with my tongue. I trailed kisses along his jaw, starting at the hinge and working down to his lightly stubbled throat. He tasted so good that I marked him above the collar before I realized what I was doing. He held my waist and pulled me tighter against him, which I took as all the invitation I needed to continue my long-awaited exploration.

The collar of his shirt impeded my progress, so I ripped it over his head with an impatient growl, revealing an expanse of pale skin decorated by even more beauty marks. Each one deserved to be lavished in attention, and I would one day, but we had all the time in the world for that.

I took a few moments to take him in and feel his skin under my palms. His chest hair was thicker than mine, but less spread out, just like the hair on his arms and legs I'd become quite familiar with. There was more than there was all those years ago, though his treasure trail was still as enticing as ever.

His body was lean and tight in a way that could only come from running. Eli had mentioned that he wanted to put on more mass, but I thought he was absolutely beautiful just as he was. I brushed my thumb over one of his dark pink nipples and he gasped, the sound deafening in the otherwise silent room. I did it again and smiled when I got the same reaction out of him.

"You're quite sensitive. That's pretty fucking sexy." I tweaked both of his nipples at once and felt his cock twitch against my stomach while he fisted the sheets and made a desperate, guttural moan. I replaced one hand with my mouth and swept my tongue over the hardened nub. His back shot up off the bed, and he cried out. I pressed him back down and held him with my free hand while I worked his nipple with my tongue, alternating between sucking and flicking over it. I bit down on it, not too hard, to see how he'd react, and almost got kicked in the balls when his whole body shook.

"Sorry," he ground out.

I used more of my weight to pin him, and went to work on his other nipple, eliciting the same enthusiastic reaction. I tortured him like that until he begged me—for more?—and choked out that he was going to come. His warning snapped some sense back into me and I released him, kissing my way back up to his mouth.

I wanted to make him come, just like I wanted to touch every part of him, but we still had so much to discuss, and we had no boundaries set. Eli wasn't gay, or at least he didn't think he was, yet there I was on the verge of making him come. The last thing I wanted was to get caught up and go too far too fast and have him regret anything we did. He deserved better than that. If I hurt him in any way it would kill me.

Eli pulled back from the kiss after a minute and stared up at me with his forehead lightly creased. "You keep holding back. Is there something wrong? Am I… doing something you don't like?"

I cupped the side of his head and traced one corner of his mouth with my thumb. "You're so incredibly sexy, and you're doing everything right. I'm trying to take it slow and not overwhelm you."

"You realize I'm not a virgin, right? I mean, I did pretty much tell you I was terrible at sex, but I have had it. With several different people." He cringed and shook off the thought. "It's been a while, but I like how you make me feel. I wish you'd touch me more."

Well, fuck. It was probably still a bad idea, but with him wanting more so openly, like hell was I going to deny him. "Will you tell me if I'm going too fast or you don't like something?"

He nodded, and I finally let go of the control I'd so desperately clung to since we reconnected. I grabbed his legs and pulled him so we were lying across the width of the bed, giving Prince a wide berth. I went for Eli's mouth again and raked my hands up and down his body while writhing against him. My hand slid down over the top of his boxers and gave his hard cock a firm squeeze. His moan was muffled by my mouth on his, and I needed to hear it in earnest. I focused on leaving another mark on his neck and gave him another squeeze, swiping my thumb over the ridge of his cockhead. He cried out, loud and sharp, and I squeezed him again.

His writhing got more frantic and his moans so sweet and low that I figured he was close. I should have left it at that and stroked him through his climax, but my greedy mouth needed to taste him. I left a trail of sloppy kisses down his torso and shimmied his boxers off, only breaking contact to slide them off over his feet.

Eli lay before me completely naked, flushed with arousal, and looking at me pleadingly. Without another moment's hesitation, I dropped down between his legs and took his uncut cock into my mouth, nearly coming undone myself in the process.

He inhaled deeply then groaned, making this primal sound that went straight to my cock. I ground my hips against the bed while I worked Eli's cock, drowning in all the beautiful sounds he made. I heard his breathing shift and knew he was close. With his fingers buried in my hair, his cock pulsed in my mouth while the rest of his body went stiff under my hands.

I swallowed everything he gave and continued to swirl my tongue over his cockhead until his body went limp and he hissed from overstimulation. I kissed each of Eli's inner thighs then crawled up and lay beside him, my fingers lightly drumming on his chest. Yeah, I was feeling pretty fucking great.

"Was that enough for you?" I asked with a shit-eating grin I couldn't keep from my face.

Eli turned his head toward me, still panting, and flashed me the happiest opened-mouth smile I'd ever seen. "Holy shit. Are you, like, really good at that or something?"

I snorted a laugh. "Excuse me?"

"I've never orgasmed that fast before," he said with a hint of embarrassment. "I usually struggle to come with a partner, but it's completely the opposite with you. So, are you some crazy sex god or something?"

Oh my God, he's being serious. "Um, I don't want to brag or anything, but I haven't received any complaints after I figured out what the hell I was doing. Maybe you just find me too irresistible," I teased.

"I definitely do." He said it so seriously, staring at me with those gorgeous brown eyes. "Would it be all right if I touched you too? I've been thinking about it for a while."

I was suddenly *very* aware of my need to come, and I fucking jumped when Eli cupped my balls. I'd been too caught up thinking about what he was asking for and didn't see his hand reach down.

"I didn't wait for an answer, but you didn't look like you were going to say no," he said with his mouth twitching into a grin.

"Fuck—do whatever you want," I ground out.

He sat up with a tired groan and slid his legs off the edge of the bed. Prince moved her head but didn't bother to get up. "Will you come stand over here for me, please?"

I did as he asked and stood between his open legs. I tried my best not to focus too closely on the sight of him sitting there—naked, and with sex hair—for fear of coming before my underwear even came off. He ran his hands up and down the front of my thighs, stopping to finger through the hair occasionally. With no hesitation he tucked his fingertips under the band of my boxers and pulled them down. My hard dick caught on the band and slapped against my stomach once freed.

Time seemed to stand still while Eli studied my cock. His hands stilled on my thighs and he just stared at me, head tilting occasionally. I had no shame surrounding my body and was fairly comfortable being naked, yet under his intense gaze I felt *bare*. Exposed. Open. Raw.

It was a strange feeling, but one I was glad only belonged to Eli. He was different from all others, and I wanted to give him everything I had, especially those parts that unnerved me. Our eyes locked as he leaned forward, so close to touching me. His hot breath ghosting over my cock was almost sensation enough to make me come. My body was starved for touch and hypersensitive; I longed for Eli in this moment more than I had any other over the past few months —more than I had for anyone in my entire life. A bead of pre-cum pooled at my slit and caught Eli's eye. He gently dabbed it with his finger and tasted it, making me whimper for more.

Watching and waiting was driving me crazy. I was liable to come from just looking into his eyes or from my eyes wandering the expanse of his gorgeous, exposed skin. Not wanting to blow before he even properly touched me, I closed my eyes and let my head drop back. With my vision obscured, the sounds and smells in the room held more of my attention.

I could hear Eli breathing, ragged and measured. I could

smell his sweat from the force and exertion of his release mixed with the scent of his lingering body wash. I heard him swallow and lick his lips then my knees nearly buckled when I felt his hot, wet tongue lick the tip of my cock.

All of the air left my lungs in an almost violent rush. My eyes squeezed shut tighter before cracking open to see Eli's lips parting around my cock, slowly taking more of it in. It had been too long and I was too turned on to last. Eli pulled off and wiped the corner of his mouth with his wrist.

"Tell me how to make this good for you," he said. He sounded so determined and focused.

I cupped his jaw and stroked his lips with my thumb before sliding it in his mouth and over the tips of his bottom teeth. I withdrew it and smeared spit over his lips, making them shine with inviting moisture. "Just go slow and don't take too much. You can use your hand to hold the base and prevent yourself from choking. Lightly sucking feels good, but your tongue will be doing most of the work. Do what feels most comfortable for you."

"I want to make you come, Bryan. And I want you to touch me."

I nodded and raked my fingers through his hair, grasping at the short strands when he took me into his mouth again. I wanted to thrust, but I kept my hips still and worked my hands through Eli's hair instead, careful not to force him farther onto my cock. He took my suggestion and held me at my base while he worked the first few inches in and out of his mouth. He readjusted his grip, adding more pressure, and pulled more of my foreskin back before taking me back in.

My toes curled, and my voice scraped out low and needy while I urged him to keep going. He kept up the pace, going faster as my breathing kicked up. His free hand held my hip hard enough that I felt his blunt nails dig into my skin. A familiar pressure began to build, and I warned him that I was going to come. He continued sucking me, and I erupted with a low moan stymied by gritted teeth. Eli backed off too soon and one last spasm shot cum on his chin. Before he could wipe it away, my mouth was on him and I swiped up the stray cum with my tongue. I broke the kiss, stroked my fingers down the front of his face, and collapsed facedown on the bed with a grunt.

Prince picked that moment to get up and attack my face. I was too weak and boneless to move and just lay there and let it happen. Eli found the scene all too amusing and laughed before taking pity on me. I heard him get up and call her from the doorway. I looked up, and he was slipping on a pullover hoodie and already had on sweats.

"I need to take Prince out for a walk. I'd invite you to come with me, but you've only got your jeans, and I've always hated how walking in jeans felt, so I figured you'd be more comfortable here." He absently scratched at his neck, drawing my eye to one of the red marks I'd left on him. Whoops.

"I'll wait here and make breakfast," I said as I sat upright. Eli's eyes traveled up and down my body, lingering on my now soft cock for a few beats before the sound of Prince's nails on the floor caught his attention.

"Right. I'll see you in twenty minutes."

They came back in fifteen minutes, just as I finished prepping vegetables and cooking bacon for omelets. By the time Eli fed Prince and washed his hands, I had breakfast hot and ready for him on the counter. He thanked me, and we ate in a comfortable silence, stealing glances at each other and smiling when we got caught.

"I suppose I don't have to be stealthy when I check you out now," I teased, pushing my empty plate away.

"I suppose not. I wish you would have told me how you

felt, though I do understand why you didn't. I'm sorry about how difficult that must have been for you." Eli lowered his plate and let Prince have the last bite of egg. He sometimes shared with her, but I was pretty sure he did it to look away from me out of guilt.

"It's all right. You didn't do anything wrong. So," I started, "is there anything you want to ask me, or do you want me to talk first?"

Without a moment's thought, Eli asked, "Am I gay?" His face was neutral and unaffected, as if he'd just asked for the time.

"Not necessarily," I said carefully. "Have you been attracted to men before?"

He shook his head. "Not at all. I'm barely attracted to anyone, but I've never even looked twice at a man before you."

He could have been bisexual, but something about that didn't seem right. "When did you start to develop feelings for me?"

Eli looked me in the eye and sat up straight. "I'm not exactly sure. It didn't just happen one day. The more I got to know you, the more I liked you, and that never stopped. There wasn't one defining incident; it's everything about you."

His voice had an air of certainty and confidence to it that I only heard when he was talking about his work, Prince, or *Star Wars*. I believed every word he said, especially after experiencing how brazen he was for his first time with a man. Well, his second. He didn't second-guess himself with his work, and that was the vibe I got from him when he spoke of his feelings for me.

I grinned at him, lacing our fingers together in his lap. "Were you physically attracted to me when we met? Um, after our misunderstanding was cleared up."

"No, not at all. I mean, I could tell you were a handsome guy, but nothing beyond that. I don't really understand how that could be, because when I look at you now, I want to tear you apart. Is that normal?"

"It's how I feel about you, too." I flashed him a small smile before continuing. "I think you might be demisexual. And likely bisexual."

"That demi thing doesn't sound normal," he mumbled.

I brought his hand up, still joined with mine, and kissed it. "You're plenty normal. All it means is that you need an emotional connection before the sex part happens. And I'm guessing bisexual because, well, here we are."

Eli's forehead creased while he thought about it, and he nodded. "It sounds accurate. It would also explain why I was such a fucking failure in all of my prior relationships."

"You weren't a failure. You didn't understand what you needed, and no one else took the time to properly find out. You didn't do anything wrong." I refused to let him go on thinking he was defective or not worthy of living life to the fullest. "I'll say it every day until you believe it."

"What if I never do?"

"Then I'll spend forever trying—if you'll have me that long," I replied.

He smiled at me then scratched the back of his head. "I don't want you to go anywhere."

"Then I won't. I meant it when I said I loved you." I looked down at Prince, lying on her side under Eli's stool. "I love both of you."

"It feels good to hear that. What do we do now? Did you want to have sex today, or…"

It was my turn to crease my forehead in confusion. "What do you think we did earlier?"

"I mean like, *sex* sex. Penetration." His confidence

wavered, and he sounded more like he did when we first met. Unsure and insecure.

"We don't have to do more, Eli. We don't have to do anything we're both not fully comfortable with. Anal sex doesn't have to be the end goal. There's no script and there are no rules—there's just us and whatever feels right."

He visibly relaxed, loosening his shoulders and easing his features. "Okay. I'd like to, just maybe not today."

"That's okay."

"I would like to blow you again, though. I think I can do better."

Fuck. "I'm not going to turn that down. Do you want to take a shower first?" The surprised look on his face morphed into intrigue and then lust. He kissed me, stroking the back of my neck then took off toward the bathroom, leaving the door open behind him.

I SPENT all of Sunday at Eli's in my underwear or less and ended up staying the night. I got up way too damn early to go to work, glad I kept a change of clothes there. The day was long and busy as usual, but the thought of Eli and the most perfect weekend kept me going strong. I had a hickey on my collarbone that served as a reminder that I hadn't dreamt the whole thing up in some lust-induced craze.

Eli's confession struck me entirely off guard, though he hadn't exactly tried to hide anything he was feeling. Mac had been hinting at it since the day he met Eli, but I was too stuck in my feelings of unrequited love and wouldn't allow myself to think he could possibly love me in return—even if *everyone* else saw it.

When I got home, Mac was blasting "Jump Around" while working in his boxers and an unzipped sweater. You know, because winter. Before I could even tell him what had happened, he jumped up with a huge shit-eating grin on his face.

"You got some! I can fucking tell—oh my God, did you tell Eli you loved him? No, not that. He told you, didn't he?"

I bit my bottom lip and smiled at him with a shrug of my shoulders. "He told me first. Why didn't you tell me, man?"

"Nah, come on. You wouldn't have believed me even if I had. You needed to hear it from him or figure it out for yourself." He stood up and rounded the island, practically bouncing toward me. "Get over here and hug me, you dense bastard," he said as he pulled me into a hug. "I'm so happy for you, Bry. For both of you. Where is our dear Elijah anyway?"

"He's at his apartment."

Mac smacked the back of my head. "Then why are you here?"

"Um, because I live here? And I wanted to see you," I replied dryly.

"I won't be offended if you leave me for Eli. Although I do still expect you to hand-deliver me baked goods every week. And, shit, the occasional dinner too."

It was my turn to whack him. "Calm down. I'm not going anywhere. Things with Eli *just* started."

"Yeah, whatever. I'll turn some music on when I go to bed, so I don't hear your kinky phone sex," he teased.

I rolled my eyes but couldn't stop myself from smiling. "Anyway, you wanna play some *COD* when you're finished working?"

He walked back over to the island and pushed his laptop closed. "The joys of working from home. Let's go."

AFTER A WEEK of rotating my nights between my apartment and Eli's, we went on our first real date. He let me plan our outing, and I thought I picked something he'd really like. On an early Saturday morning I made raspberry pancakes with a peach schnapps reduction for breakfast in bed—which also turned into mutual blowjobs—before we got dressed and caught a bus. I'd mentioned a cab, but Eli insisted we could take the bus or train, depending on the distance, and cut down on the cost.

Eli wasn't a man entertained by grand, expensive gestures, so when we arrived at the Adler planetarium and I saw his surprised, wide-eyed expression, I knew I'd made the correct choice. I gave myself a mental high five when he smiled at me and said he'd never been there before.

I paid for our admission and Eli kept quiet until we were out of earshot from the ticket clerk. He asked me why I paid for him, and I simply told him it was because we were on a date.

"Does that make me the girl, then? I mean, in terms of how our roles work. I always paid when I took girls out. It was expected."

I stopped our progression and pulled him aside, out of the way of a family behind us. "Absolutely not. There isn't a male-female dynamic here. I paid for you because I'm taking you out. If you want to take me out and pay, you can. Or we can split it if you're more comfortable with that. Remember what I said before? There are no rules—it's just us and whatever we want."

"I'm sorry. I'm ruining this."

I cupped his cheek and kissed his forehead. "You're not. Now come on. There's a ton of cool stuff I want you to see today."

We started in the Welcome Gallery, taking in the kaleidoscope of colors and the shadows we cast along the walls.

Halfway through, Eli asked if it would be strange for us to hold hands. My reply came in the form of taking his hand in mine and planting a kiss on each of his fingers.

All of the exhibits and shows were interesting, but we both enjoyed the Skywatch one best. Sitting in the quiet, dark auditorium and seeing the stars over Chicago while we held hands was an incredible experience. He told me he felt so small and insignificant in the grand scheme, and while I knew it to be true in a literal sense, it wasn't how I felt with him. I gently pressed my lips to his and whispered that we were princes of the universe and could have whatever we wanted. He liked that.

Eli wanted to stop in the gift shop on our way out and kept coming back to a mug set that said, "To the Moon and Back." We ended up going splits on them and agreed to keep them in our respective workplaces to commemorate our first date and to serve as reminders of each other when we couldn't be together.

When Monday morning came, I read the instructions for that fancy-as-hell coffeemaker, brewed myself a cup, and used my brand-new mug, smiling all the while like the lovesick fool I was.

SEVENTEEN

ELI

I WORE A ZIP-UP HOODIE TO WORK IN an attempt to hide the hickies Bryan liked to leave on my neck so much. I couldn't lie; I liked them too, but the amused looks from my colleagues made me extremely uncomfortable. I handled Eve's playful ribbing, but having my other colleagues know what I was up to bothered me. I wanted Bryan all to myself and them knowing I had *someone*—even if they didn't know it was him—felt too much like sharing. I didn't know I was a greedy person, but then again, there were a lot of things I didn't know about myself.

When I strolled into work the Monday after Bryan and I got together, I'd forgotten about the marks on my neck and sat down at my desk, completely oblivious to the curious looks. I had new marks on my neck and chest from after our date the other day.

There was always a battle over the thermostat in the wintertime, and it was cranked up to the max. After working for an hour, I began to sweat and mindlessly unzipped my sweater. Eve popped her head up and casually asked how my weekend went.

"It was really good. Bryan made me these yummy pancakes and took me to the planetarium on Saturday. We had a lot of fun."

"Sure look it," she replied with a knowing grin.

I furrowed my brow and tilted my head in question. "What?"

She motioned to her neck, and my face paled. I reached across the desk and grabbed her mirror, cringing when I saw the deep burgundy and purple marks on both sides of my neck. "Fucking hell," I said as I zipped the sweater back up.

"No one cares about the marks, pet. They all know you've found someone; no need to hide them now."

"Does everyone really know?" I looked around then lowered my voice and continued, "Do they know it's Bryan? Some people might see that as a conflict of interest."

She waved a hand to dismiss the notion. "No, no one knows who, and they know better than to ask. As for a conflict, everything started after the job was finished. You've got nothing to worry about. Try to relax and be happy. And maybe tell Bryan to keep his love bites to where the rest of the world can't see," she added with a wink.

Maybe I'd return the favor and let Mac tease him when we headed over for Thanksgiving dinner in a week. I was eager to spend a holiday with Bryan. We both had a long weekend we were looking forward to spending together in varying states of undress, as he'd worded it. I wondered if he'd want to have sex soon. It had only been a few weeks, but I could imagine that he had to want it. I could hear his voice in my head telling me that there were no rules, and I tried not to think about it. At least for a little while longer.

"Can I just say that I saw this coming? Back in August, no

less. You two are so clueless," Mac said with a rather triumphant smile in place.

Bryan shook his head and snorted from behind the kitchen counter as he put the finishing touches on our delicious-smelling Thanksgiving dinner. I sat at the kitchen table with Mac playing—and losing miserably—a game of cribbage. It was a new game to me, though the rules were simple enough. I hadn't quite mastered the art of splitting my hand, but Bryan and Mac told me it came with time.

Bryan announced that dinner was ready and took our game board and cards away before I could get skunked, much to Mac's displeasure. In a rare display, Mac was fully clothed, albeit in a tank and pajama bottoms. The game was replaced with three hot dishes holding shepherd's pie, carved-up turkey meat, and oven-roasted Brussels sprouts. The gravy came over last with two bottles of red wine. Bryan took a seat between us, and we enjoyed a dinner full of great food, laughs, and Mac's cheesy throwback party music.

One of Bryan's brothers had called him a few days ago, asking if he'd be coming home for dinner, but he opted to spend it here with Mac and me. He said he might be home for Christmas if it was what *we* wanted to do. Being included in his decision-making like that was one of the little things that made our relationship feel different than how it previously was. We still watched movies on my couch more than anything, only now we got to do it in our underwear and without having to worry about whether we were revealing too much.

With dinner cleared away and my stomach so full I thought I might die, Bryan brought over a gorgeous white frosted cake adorned with walnuts and maybe sprinkled cinnamon. I welcome death after tasting the first bite of what turned out to be carrot *and* pumpkin cake with cream cheese frosting. I managed to contain myself, but Mac was uninhibited in making moans that bordered on pornographic.

Bryan suggested a game before he and I departed to go back to Prince, and Mac immediately jumped up and shouted, "Truth or drink."

So we played truth or drink—but with half and quarter shots instead of full ones. I learned some pretty embarrassing things about Bryan, like that he used to let Mac's little sister use him as a dress-up doll and attend tea parties—*and* there was photo evidence at Mac's house. There was more truth-telling than drinking going on, which reminded me of how close they truly were and how thankful I was to be a part of that.

Mac drew his next card and grinned wolfishly at me. "This one's for Eli. Describe in detail how you lost your virginity." He flicked the card onto the discard pile and watched me with amusement in his eyes.

Dread crept through my body, making me go stiff. Before I could stop myself, I glanced over at Bryan and knew he noticed the change in me. I took a deep breath and tried for the illusion of acting casual.

"Um, fuck. I…" I wanted to drink the whole fucking bottle, but forgoing the answer would only draw attention to why I didn't want to answer the question. "It was with an older woman," I started. I told them a true story about how I was seduced by my boss in her office after work one evening. I followed the story with a full shot.

"An older woman—how spicy. Why were you so reluctant to say? Don't tell me it was for Bryan's sensibilities." Mac's tone was light, and he was completely unaware of what that simple question brought back for me.

"I, uh, was twenty-one when it happened."

The room fell silent after that admission. Mac turned to Bryan, and the two had a wordless exchange before Mac got up and awkwardly excused himself to his room. I forced myself to meet Bryan's eyes and the shock there told me he knew what I was about to say.

"Eli—"

"It's exactly what you're thinking, Bryan. Please don't make me say it." My voice sounded hollow to my ears. The night I tried so hard not to think about replayed in my mind. I had been an eighteen-year-old virgin in need of quick money after my mom died. I was desperate and felt like I had no other options when I agreed to do fucking porn.

Rhett—Bryan—had eased my nerves somewhat prior, but when filming started I wanted to scream. I had a feeling it would hurt, but I was ill-prepared for just how much it did. I somehow managed to keep from screaming and making a scene during each of the takes until the director said we were finished.

"I'm so sorry. I didn't know. I thought you were—" He snapped his jaw shut, and the shock in his eyes turned into regret. "'It's my first time.' You told me, and I… I thought you meant filming. God, Elijah, I'm so sorry."

Bryan reached for my hand, and I reflexively flinched, before I could even register that it was him. I was wound way too tight from thinking about that awful day. The Bryan sitting before me had nothing to do with that, and seeing his face fall when I'd pulled away from him made me feel worse.

I took his hand and squeezed it to make sure I had his attention. "I'm sorry I pulled away. It has nothing to do with you; it's just my go-to when I'm stressed out." I started to say more then cut myself off and glanced down the hall. "Mac knows, doesn't he?"

"Yes," Bryan answered quietly. "I told him about meeting you at the shoot back then, and then again when I found you by chance."

I nodded, processing that information. "Has he seen it?"

His lips twitched before he answered, and I already knew that he was going to say yes. "Yes. Several times years ago. No one else you've met has."

I puffed my cheeks and released a deep breath. Getting all of that out between us made me feel lighter. I was still low-key freaking out about *how* it came out, but I was glad that it finally did. Maybe now I'd be able to work past it.

Bryan looked like he was about to pass out or throw up when I finally replied with simply, "Okay."

"Okay, what?"

"I'm okay," I reiterated. "I mean, other people knowing isn't ideal, but I don't want to freak out and retreat over this. I have no reason to run from you, and I'm tired of running from the situation." Bryan looked like he didn't believe me when I mentioned him, so I wanted to make it clear. "You don't have to feel sorry about what happened. I was eighteen, and I fully agreed to everything that happened that day."

He ground his teeth before asking, "Did I hurt you?"

I couldn't—wouldn't—lie, even if I thought it would be easier on him. I knew he'd do the same for me. "It hurt, yes. Quite a bit. That experience was why I was so certain I wasn't attracted to men. I considered the possibility that maybe I was gay as an explanation for why I didn't care about girls the way other guys did—but I didn't care about sex with *any*one."

Bryan brought our joined hands up and kissed mine, his forehead still creased with concern. "I'm sorry I didn't notice. I wouldn't have gone ahead with it had I known."

"It's all right. I-I needed that money for Prince and me. I had nothing, Bryan. Believe me when I say that nothing that happened that day was your fault. It would have happened regardless, but I'm glad it was with you." His face twisted, and I could tell he didn't understand my logic. "For whatever reason, I left an impression on you. If that hadn't happened between us, you probably wouldn't have cared about me when you walked through the door at Red Right Hand. We wouldn't have become friends, and I wouldn't know what it means to love someone like I love you. My life hasn't always been easy, but I wouldn't change anything that happened to me if it meant I wouldn't be here with you now."

He blinked away tears that almost fell and cupped the back of my head, curling his fingers gently into my hair. I didn't wait for him to guide me—I leaned in to claim his mouth in a kiss I hoped showed how much I cared for him. He returned the message loud and clear, nipping at my bottom lip and my jaw. A low moan fell from my lips before I pulled back and nodded down the hall.

"Um, I'd like to continue this further, but maybe another time?"

Bryan followed my gaze to Mac's door and dropped his forehead to my shoulder. "Shit. Of course."

"You can text Mac that it's safe to come back out. We have a game to finish, and I want to apologize for lying."

"You don't have to do that," Bryan responded, stroking his thumbs over the sensitive underside of my wrist.

"I know—but I should."

Bryan got up and kissed the spot on my wrist he'd just been massaging. "I love you so much." He sighed and released my hand. "Let me go get Mac before he bores himself to death."

BRYAN INSISTED on taking Prince out alone when we arrived back at my place. I waited in my room, eyeing the painted canvases in my closet. I chose earth tones that reminded me of Bryan in all but one piece, which was an unfinished abstract self-portrait. The strokes in that one were hesitant and disjointed, whereas all of the ones that represented Bryan were painted with confidence and certainty. I knew how he made me feel and how I felt about him; following through on those strokes was easy. I considered myself a work in progress, but I was looking forward to figuring it all out instead of stagnating and convincing myself I was happy.

Meeting Bryan showed me just how unhappy and alone I was before. He brought so much light and energy to my world just by being around. I loved him for knowing when to push my limits, and when I needed a break. My anxiety would probably be something I dealt with for a long time to come, but I had no doubts that I would slowly continue to improve.

The front door opened and the telltale sound of nails clicking closed in on the bedroom. I closed the closet door and walked around the bed to see my sweet girl.

Bryan joined us, crossing his arms across his chest and leaning against the doorframe. I smiled at him, which he returned half-heartedly. I knew he had to be beating himself up over my revelation earlier, but that was the last thing I wanted. That night was another lifetime ago and what mattered was the present. I needed him to understand that.

I kissed Prince's forehead and told her to go lie down on the couch. Once she left the room, I asked Bryan to close the door and sat down on the bed, patting the spot next to me. He joined me without a word.

"I grew up very poor and didn't know my father," I started, grabbing Bryan's attention. "My mom did her best for me, but she had her own troubles. She didn't go out very much and didn't have many friends, nor did I. Except for when I went to school, I didn't interact with hardly anyone else.

"In my last year of high school, I got a scholarship to UIC and a part-time job to buy a cheap, used car to commute from the dorms to home to see Mom. She always smoked in the house, and I constantly reminded her not to smoke in bed, or would check on her after she fell asleep to make sure she put her cigarettes out. She fell asleep with one lit while I was at school and died in a house fire when I was eighteen."

Bryan hooked his hand around my inner thigh, just above my knee, and squeezed. "Eli, God, that's horrible."

I nodded and swallowed, despite my throat being dry. He needed to know everything. "After she died, I was all alone, and I panicked. I dropped out of school and lost my scholarship and found myself homeless with nowhere and no one to turn to. Turns out she didn't have home insurance, let alone life insurance.

"I lived out of my car for a couple weeks and found Prince abandoned in the street. She was underweight and too young to be away from her mother, so I took her to the vet. The cost of her vet bills is why I was desperate enough to agree when I was approached about the shoot. It was just supposed to be me jerking off on camera for five hundred bucks. Easy, right?

"When the producer offered me more for having sex on camera, I said yes. No one coerced me, and no one forced me. It was a shitty situation, and I did what I had to do. That money was enough to help Prince. I had enough left over for us to eat for a few weeks, and get myself cleaned up. I got a job after that and was soon able to rent a small apartment and start rebuilding. Without that money, I don't know what would have happened." I took his hands in mine and took a deep breath so my next words would come out steady. "While I don't regret it, the act itself is a bad memory. But we're not those people anymore. You're not Rhett, and I'm not desperate. I've lived long enough carrying that memory around, and I want to overwrite it with a good one."

Bryan furrowed his brow, and I could tell my intent wasn't as transparent as I'd hoped. I leaned into his space, slid a hand around the back of his neck, and kissed him. When he broke away, I licked my lips, savoring the sweet taste of him. "I want you to fuck me. Er, that's not romantic. I want you in every way, and I want that last bit of physical connection with you. When I think about you and sex, I want to remember tonight and how amazing it was. I want you to have every part of me." I stared at him, waiting for an answer that took too long to come. "Say something, Bryan."

"Are you sure you want this?" His voice scraped out, just above a whisper.

"I am. I'm hoping you do too."

"I always want you, Eli. Always. You're everything I've always wanted, and I'd be honored to give you good memories for as long as you want them from me."

I smiled and kissed him again, swinging my leg over his and settling in his lap. I surprised myself with how quickly I took to sex with Bryan compared to how awkward and unenjoyable I'd always found it. The intimacy we shared, even in the simplest of acts, carried over to our sex lives, and it felt like the most natural thing in the world to me.

Bryan slid his hands up my thighs and around to cup my ass while he kissed and licked my neck, driving me crazy with the friction from his scruff. I was about to lose my mind when he suddenly stopped and groaned.

"I didn't bring any condoms."

Oh, right. "Um, I haven't had any here for a couple of years—that was the last time for me." I bit my lip and nervously said, "I'm pretty sure I don't have anything. I haven't been to the doctor in over a year, but I was clean then and I haven't touched anyone until you." My ears burned, matching the flush I'm sure was present on my face.

"If you're suggesting what I think you're suggesting, I get

tested every three months. September was the last time, but I haven't hooked up with anyone since July… before I found you." He brushed his thumb across my cheek then over the corner of my mouth.

"I haven't had sex without a condom before."

"Neither have I," he replied.

I was almost too nervous to speak. I managed to force my next words out. "Are we really going to do this?"

His reply came in the form of tightening his grip on my ass and rising to his feet. "Shower first, love."

This is really happening, was all that ran through my mind as my head hit the pillow. My dampened, bare skin was cold in the bedroom air, but I knew I'd have Bryan's warmth soon. He knelt above me, reaching into the nightstand for the small bottle of lube he bought when he showed me what frotting was—something I would *never* forget.

He tossed the bottle near the pillows then lowered himself over me, going straight for my neck, just below my ear in a spot that made me squirm. We both discovered so many new sensitive spots on my body I hadn't known existed, and Bryan put all of that into practice as he pinched my nipple and rubbed his hard cock against mine. The drag without lube bordered on being not enough, but I'd discovered that Bryan liked to tease and would always give me more if I was patient.

His kisses trailed up along my jaw before finding my lips and letting me feast on that sweet taste that was so distinctly Bryan. His familiar smell was largely masked by my body wash, but when I closed my eyes and breathed him in, I caught subtle hints of vanilla and citrus. That same smell that had comforted me for months, that represented someone I never wanted to be without. I wrapped my arms around his neck and chased after more of the scent, for more of him.

I caught his earlobe between my teeth and tugged, hard enough to make him wince and pin my hands above my head. He kissed down my body, focusing on each sensitive spot as he'd done countless times these past weeks, though he ignored my cock entirely. I felt his lips and tongue on my inner thighs and his nose against my balls, but nothing where I wanted him most. I was about to beg when he grabbed the pillow next to my head, bent my legs back from behind my knees, and stuffed the pillow under my ass. It all happened so quickly, and I was lying there with my ass on display and a deep flush creeping up my neck.

"What are you doing?" I croaked out.

He wrapped his arms around my thighs, pushing them farther back and grinned up at me. "I'm about to get a taste of your cake."

What? I opened my mouth to ask what the hell he meant when his tongue darted out and swept across my fucking asshole. I cried out in shock, alarmed at the act itself, but more specifically how *good* it felt. He did it again, eliciting another moan from me I couldn't begin to hold in. What he was doing seemed wrong and taboo, but it felt so fucking good.

My hands fisted his hair as he flicked his tongue over my hole, occasionally tracing my perineum and tonguing my balls. I was on the verge of coming when he slowed down and replaced his tongue with his thumb, gently pressing against my resistance.

"Pass me the lube," he drawled, voice thick with lust.

I flailed my arm, blindly looking for it. I couldn't break my eye contact with him, even if it did prolong my simple task by a couple of seconds that felt like an eternity. I found the bottle and handed it to him, only then letting my head drop back and closing my eyes. The click of the bottle opening and the viscous slide of slicked fingers rubbing

together reached my ears, making my cock twitch in anticipation.

At the same time Bryan's lips closed around my cockhead, his thumb circled my hole. I sucked in a sharp breath
as my hips jutted up, seeking more of the wet heat of Bryan's
mouth. He held me down with his free hand and chuckled.
The vibrations from his laughter created an exquisite sensation on my cock, making me shiver. He swirled his tongue
around me and pressed harder against me with one of his
fingers.

My cock slid out of his mouth, and I held my head back
up to see what was happening. Bryan licked his lips and kept
rubbing. "This is going to feel strange at first, and it will
probably hurt when I add more fingers, but I promise it will
get better."

I nodded and let my head fall back, bracing for pain.

"You have to relax, Eli. This won't work if you're tense,"
Bryan said in a soothing voice. He licked my cock from root
to tip and took it in his mouth, all the way down till I hit the
back of his throat. My whole body went lax, and I moaned,
low and deep. His finger slid inside me then, drawing
another sharp gasp from me.

It didn't hurt, but it felt strange. He kept his finger still
while continuing to bob his head up and down on my cock
while I adjusted to the intrusion. I was about to come again
when he slowed down and began sliding his finger in and out
of me. There still wasn't any pain, but it didn't feel great
either. His finger moved in a few different directions and
depths on each plunge until he touched something that made
me grit my teeth to keep from screaming. He laughed again,
seemingly pleased with himself and stroked that spot inside
me over and over. It was unlike anything else he'd done to
me. The feeling was so intense and far reaching, sending
waves of pleasure throughout my whole body.

He clicked open the lube again and drizzled more where we were connected before he slid a second finger slowly inside me. *Then* I felt a burn. I felt stretched and open and it hurt, but not enough to ask him to stop. He rubbed that sensitive spot inside me and sucked on my cockhead, making the burn fade into the background.

Bryan kept up the dual assault until I was on the edge again, begging and pleading for release. Without stopping, he worked a third finger inside me and I reflexively tightened around his fingers, wincing from the stretch.

"Breathe, Elijah." Bryan sucked each of my balls into his mouth, rolling them over his tongue one at a time while keeping his fingers still. "Tell me when I can move them," he said before going back to lavishing my balls with his tongue.

I took deep, measured breaths until the throb in my ass faded a bit, then told Bryan I was ready for more. He added even more lube to the mix and slowly worked his fingers in as far as they could go then slid them out almost entirely again and again.

My pained sighs turned into pleasurable ones before I'd realized it, then Bryan's fingers were gone. I felt his absence in me and almost craved to have that pressure back. He licked me from root to tip as he crawled up my body until our mouths were aligned. He hesitated to kiss me, so I made the decision for him and angled my head up to connect our lips in a slow, sensuous kiss. Our tongues collided while his fingers intertwined with mine against the bed.

"Are you sure you want this?" he whispered against my lips.

I nodded, but he insisted I say it. "I want this. I want you."

He kissed me again then sat up and squeezed more lube onto his cock, sliding his free hand over his length until he was slicked up and ready. He rubbed more against me then lined up his cock, gently pressing the blunt tip against my hole. It felt like a lot; a whole lot more than his fingers. I swallowed hard and peered down at where we were about to be joined as doubt crept into the edges of my mind.

"Is this going to work?" I asked nervously.

Bryan placed his hand on my chest and motioned for me to do the same. "Do you feel that?" he asked. His heart pounded under my hand, just as mine did under his. "I'm just as nervous as you. We don't have to do this today, but if you still want to, please trust me. It's going to hurt more than my fingers did, but it will pass, I promise you that."

"Okay," I choked out.

He smiled down at me then slowly pushed in, stopping halfway when I winced and my hands flew to his thighs, gripping him tight. His uneven voice urged me to breathe and relax. He sounded winded almost, and I realized that it probably took a lot of restraint for him to go this slow on my account. I studied his face and saw lines of concentration on his forehead and the muscles in his jaw flinch, telling me his teeth were clenched. I focused on him and his reactions as he pushed farther in until his body was pressed up against mine. His mouth grew slack and his lips trembled as he stared back at me, making me hot all over.

My ass stung and burned, but it wasn't anywhere near the pain I remembered from years ago. I was still hard, just from watching the enjoyment play out across his features. I reached for him, craving his warmth, and he leaned down over me, taking my mouth as he slowly ground his hips into me.

I cried out into his mouth and wrapped my arms under his, latching onto his back. His muscles moved under my fingers with every controlled thrust, and I wondered how beautiful that would be to see. The thought of *watching* as Bryan and I did this made my skin prickle to attention.

He snapped his hips a little harder and nailed that sensitive spot. The pain from the sudden movement was far outweighed by the almost overwhelming pleasure from his cock stimulating that spot. The burn persisted, but his thrusts kept hitting their target, and I stopped caring about the pain. We both panted and moaned, each giving and taking from each other all we could. Bryan slid a hand between us and stroked my cock in time with his quickening thrusts, tearing apart the last threads of my self-control.

My orgasm started at the base of my spine and roared through me with more force than I ever thought possible. My body felt like it had been disassembled and reconfigured at the molecular level and now permanently had a part of Bryan within me. My voice came out strangled and hoarse from overuse as I dug my blunt nails into the smooth skin on his back. He kept moving, fucking me through my spasms until he stilled and his breaths stuttered out as his cock pulsed inside me.

He collapsed on top of me, burrowing his face into the crook of my neck, nipping at my sensitive skin. His hand came up and brushed my sweat-dampened hair back from my forehead, and he trailed soft, sweet kisses all over my neck, like he couldn't get enough of the taste. I was too exhausted to lift my head and kiss him back, so I lay there, chest heaving and ragged.

When both of our breathing leveled out, Bryan pressed his forehead to mine and smiled, asking if I was okay. I simply returned his warm smile and nodded, not yet able to form coherent sentences. He sat up and slowly pulled out of me, and I winced at his absence in and around me. His fingers smeared the drying cum on his stomach, and he suggested we take another shower. A grunt was all I could muster. He snorted a laugh and rolled off the bed and left the room. I heard him scream when Prince must have attacked him and rolled on my side, snickering.

WE LET Prince back into the bedroom after we showered again. She acted like she hadn't seen us in weeks, and I felt mildly guilty for having locked her out. Bryan sat behind me with his arms around my waist, hiding his head against my back while she tried to get at his face. Although I really couldn't blame her.

In the shower, Bryan had told me again that he loved me while he cleaned me up. I was still unsteady on my feet and had relied on him to keep me upright, which he did without me needing to ask. When we got back to my room, I told him I wanted to show him something and led him over to the closet. I opened the door and let him look through the painted canvases and at the larger, unpainted one. I'd thanked him for inspiring me to paint again and asked if he'd model for the larger piece, to which he enthusiastically agreed.

We'd moved to the bed, where Bryan had started kissing me and feeling me up again when Prince jumped up and attacked him. We moved to the head of the bed, where we sat now, and I laughed as he protested Prince's relentless brand of love.

"You might as well give in. She'll never give up until she gets her way."

He held me tighter and *giggled* adorably against the back of my neck. "I can wait her out forever if I have to."

"You'll starve to death before she stops," I teased.

"I've finally feasted on the best cake of all and can die happy. Bring it."

I turned my head back toward him and asked what he

meant, and he shifted one hand down and squeezed my ass. "This cake right here," he drawled into my ear.

My eyes went wide as realization struck. "Oh my God, the bakery…"

He broke out into laughter, spurring Prince on even more. "You really didn't know what that meant?"

"I'm so fucking clueless," I mumbled.

"Maybe, but I still love you."

I echoed the words back to him, and he kissed my cheek before he released his hold on me and let Prince have her way with him. I turned and looked on as the two things I valued most in the world were happy and healthy, and I considered myself lucky beyond measure. I was lucky to have found Bryan and lucky to have this chance at a new beginning. I intended to make the most of my good fortune every day going forward.

EPILOGUE

BRYAN

Six Months Later

I COULDN'T RECALL A TIME IN MY LIFE when I was happier than I was now. Business held steady over the winter and significantly picked up with the onset of spring— I was even able to hire more staff and reduce my own hours so I could see Eli more. Speaking of, he and I were taking the next step and moving in together in a few days. Mac gave me hell about having called it back in November, but he was supportive of us and had been waiting for us to "pull our heads out of our asses."

The timing was pretty handy to help out a friend too. Eve's younger brother got evicted from his apartment and had been crashing with her and Samir, causing some friction for the newlyweds. I talked to Mac first then offered my old room for Dubhlainn to rent at a reduced rate. I owned the apartment, so it wasn't a big deal or adding any financial burden to Mac. As a thank-you to my best friend, I was spending my Sunday evening at the bakery with Eli making croissants, macarons, and a red velvet cake to bring over the next day.

As great as everything had been going, a little something I'd been carrying around for three weeks made me feel anxiety like nothing else ever had. It was a smooth platinum band with a small brown topaz stone that matched Eli's eyes; it was an engagement ring. I'd bought it while I was out looking for earrings for my mom for Mother's Day and had kept it on my person ever since for fear of Eli finding it before I was ready.

I knew without a doubt that I wanted to commit the rest of my life to him, but I wanted the proposal to be perfect. Finding that perfect moment where life didn't get in the way was far more difficult than I thought it would be. I obsessed over how to propose some nights to the point where it kept me up for hours.

A loud clang caught my attention, and I craned my neck to see that Eli had dropped an empty mixing bowl on the floor. He cursed under his breath and picked it up, setting it aside and grabbing a new one. He'd borrowed one of my aprons and looked more like a snack instead of a chef. Knowing and not caring that I'd have to start over, I abandoned the dough I'd been kneading at my station and crept up behind Eli. I placed a hand on his hip, startling him. He turned his head then relaxed into my hold when he saw me.

"What are you up to?" he asked suspiciously.

I hummed in response and slid my hands up under the hem of his shirt, leaving a trail of flour everywhere my hands touched. I skimmed over his ticklish ribs, his chest, and tight stomach. He sucked in a sharp breath when I roughly brushed a nipple with my thumb, so I did it again. I wasn't planning on taking things further than some mild groping, but when he rested his head against my shoulder and moaned while grinding his ass into my crotch, my self-restraint frayed and snapped.

I'd unbuttoned his pants and worked my hand into his underwear when I realized that this, in its own way, was a perfect moment; every moment with Eli was new and exciting and *perfect*. Whether we were fighting, fucking, cooking, or watching a movie, it was all perfect because of him.

I didn't need to wait for the stars to align or for the sunset to be just right. All that mattered was us. No flair, no gimmicks, and no bullshit. It was just like I'd been telling him: there were no rules. I'd momentarily lost sight of that and wasted too much time fretting. Without a doubt, I knew he'd say yes, and I wanted to ask him as soon as possible—just not in the middle of sex. I doubted he'd ever forgive me for that, and I planned on being in his good graces forever.

ALSO BY SERENE FRANKLIN

ACKNOWLEDGMENTS

Special thanks are in order for a few people. First up are Cass and Jenny for alpha reading once again.

To Katze for always listening, being supportive, and helping keep me focused.

To Caitlyn for putting up with my rants, and for always indulging me when I go off on a tangent about my boys. Oh, and for "Fat Bottomed Girls".

To Steven for making Chicago feel like a second home.

ABOUT THE AUTHOR

Serene Franklin lives in Halifax (Nova Scotia, not California), but has fallen in love with Chicago through research and writing. She has a political science degree, and—more importantly—an adorable and mildly irritating Goldendoodle named Tai.

When not writing, she enjoys reading, cooking spicy food, thrashing to music, losing at crib, and watching movies. Serene is a proud otaku and collector of anime figures in addition to novels and yaoi manga.

Serene currently writes contemporary MM romance, but has plans to branch out into other subgenres.

Email: sfwrites801@gmail.com

 twitter.com/serenitydarko

 instagram.com/serenity_darko

 bookbub.com/profile/serene-franklin

www.ingramcontent.com/pod-product-compliance
Lightning Source LLC
Chambersburg PA
CBHW032124170626
46808CB00006B/2101